# ADVANCE PRAISE FOR *WARM ARCTIC NIGHTS*

To read this story of a young adolescent living through the atrocities of the Nazis and fleeing the barbarism of war, is to open a portal to the work of one of the most fearless writers of our times, too long working in obscurity. He turned from his native Ukrainian to reinvent the English language. This work stands with Nabokov, with Imre Kertesz, as a revelation in a disaster, and Tarnawsky's works expose our language to the passion and inventions of a structural magician.

— Steve Katz, author of *The Exaggerations of Peter Prince* and *The Compleat Memoirrhoids*

By turns reminiscent of Zweig's *The World of Yesterday* and Kosinsky's *The Painted Bird*, Yuriy Tarnawsky's *Warm Arctic Nights* is a swift and deeply engrossing fictive memoir of an idyllic childhood whose martial and masculine tenets presage an onslaught of inhumanity and fear. Steeped in subtle irony and the surreal, it is also a sui generis act of remembrance, memorial, and love.

—Michael Mejia, author of *TOKYO* and *Forgetfulness*

Long after having read *Warm Arctic Nights* you are left with a shudder of emotion and nostalgia, as after hearing a piano sonata by Beethoven, nerves impregnated with its strains. The writing of Yuriy Tarnawsky has that ever rarer quality of a poetic language, the intensity and purity of which renders his stories unforgettable. This particular story, imbued with his childhood years, is unlike the previous novels with their delightful dimension of the fantastic—here, cruelly, almost unbearably honest, we are given a self-portrait of the artist which will not be forgotten.

— Alain Arias-Misson, author of *Autobiography of a Character from Fiction* and *The Man Who Walked on Air*

YURIY TARNAWSKY

# WARM ARCTIC NIGHTS

## A NOVEL

2019

Cover Design by Norman Conquest
Author Photo by Oleh Holovackij

ISBN 1-884097-83-9
ISBN-13 978-1-884097-83-6

ISSN 1084-547X

This volume is volume 83 of
*The Journal of Experimental Fiction*

JEF Books/Depth Charge Publishing
Aurora, Illinois

JEF Books/Depth Charge Publishing
The Foremost in Innovative Fiction
Experimentalfiction.com

JEF Books are distributed
to the book trade by SPD: Small Press Distribution
and to the academic journal market by EBSCO

*To the memory of my father*
*who loved me more*
*than anyone else*

# Aria

---

*Schlaf, Kindchen, schlaf!*
*Dein Vater ist ein Graf.*
*Deine Mutter ist eine Edelfrau.*
*Sie badet dich im Morgentau.*
*Schlaf, Kindchen, schlaf!*

# PART ONE

---

# WARM

# 1

------

*How was the room?*

It was long and narrow, with a tall ceiling, filled with the rose and honey light of a kerosene lamp, shadows along its walls looking like rows of tall men dressed in long black robes, stern-looking, but kindly disposed toward me. They would nod approvingly as I was bathed, before being put to bed, in a sit-up zinc tub in warm water, turned light brown from the oak bark steeped in it which made my skin squeak. Sometimes, mint was steeped in it instead and its fresh smell accompanied me to the cozy world of my bed.

There was a big soft moss-green tufted sofa against one of the walls, a huge wardrobe of shiny varnished straw-colored wood along another one, and a big round table in the middle, covered with a dark green velvet cloth that in places reached to the floor. I loved to hide under it, pretending to be in a tent looking out for Indians who were coming to scalp me, at whom I was going to shoot a long wooden pen with its sharp steel point dipped in red ink to make it poisonous, using a bow I had made myself.

In the evening, father would walk around it with a furrowed brow, his head bent down and arms crossed behind his back, engrossed in thoughts, while I watched him as I lay on the sofa. They'd dress me in night clothes if I wasn't wearing them already and had fallen asleep and would put me to bed without my waking up. It was nice to wake up in the morning cuddled by the soft down comforter inside its white case.

*A psyche mirror?*

It was in my parents' bedroom, where I also slept, part of a dresser of shiny varnished straw-colored wood that went with the wardrobe in the big room and with my parents' big bed and the two night tables that stood on both sides of it.

The drawers on the right of the mirror went up higher than those on the left and there was a little platform between them on which I would climb up and do things while watching myself in the mirror. When you tipped it one way, you could see more of your feet, and the other way—the ceiling above your head.

*What was the room in?*

Inside a long single-storied stucco building with a green metal roof. Our apartment took up most of the building while the rest was occupied by the office in which father spent much of his time during the day. Big blackcurrant bushes grew along its long front wall in which I in turn spent much of my time while playing outside. The strong, winy smell of their leaves

4

has stayed in my memory to this day like a wisp of smoke hanging still in the air.

*Where was the building located?*

At a manor estate consisting of a park overgrown with huge old trees which was crisscrossed by roads covered with hard-packed yellow sand and had marble statues of human figures, some naked, other dressed, standing along them in places. It was filled with the singing of birds, which you could never see because they were high up in the trees. It seemed there were deep puddles of beautiful sounds high up among the leaves and the birds were bathing in them, splashing them with their wings as they washed, so that they fell in drops to the ground.

The park was surrounded by a tall brick wall covered with stucco, and the manor house stood in the middle of it, with a wide lawn in front. The building we lived in was on the other side of the lawn facing the manor house, along a circular drive cutting through it.

*What was the manor house like?*

Big, two-storied, made of brick and stucco and under a tall red-tiled roof, with a portico in front that carriages and cars could drive under and a single-story wing on each of the two sides. An open gallery ran along the middle of the main facade on the second floor which connected to a terrace on the right with a balustrade around it. There were palm trees growing in huge pots along the gallery and on the terrace, and rhododendron bushes on the ground along the two wings.

Inside, there was a long corridor with doors leading to rooms on the right and left and windows on each of the ends. The floor was covered with black marble tiles on which the light from the window you faced reflected, making it look like it was checkered black and white.

*Who lived in the manor house?*

*Hrabia*—count—Karol and his family as well as the servants. There was his wife, *hrabina*—countess—Apolinaria, his sister Anna, and the two teenage identical twin sons Karol Adam and Karol Bogdan, called Adek and Bodek, respectively. Adek came into the world half an hour before Bodek and played the role of the elder brother which Bodek accepted without any protest as if it were the natural thing to do. The two were away most of the time, as they went to school in a big city, but would often come home even for short holidays and spent entire summers at the estate.

*What about horses?*

In addition to work horses, there were a few for riding, maybe seven or eight. The hrabia's horse was a big bay called Marszałek, the hrabina's—a small white mare Marysia, a beautiful dappled horse father rode called Tarant, but also often Jan Amor, and the two boys' chestnut horses, Adek's and

Bodek's, called, respectively, Stan and Ollie after the movie comedians the boys were crazy about. (They would be gone sometimes for a couple of days in order to see one of their movies if they learned it was playing in some far-away city.) There was also a short-legged, long-maned dun Shetland pony called Wee Jerzyk that was used mostly to pull a little two-wheeled carriage, which I was sometimes permitted to ride on. The two boys had spent some time in England at a school and often spoke English to each other, which no one understood. It was they who had named the pony.

*Nora?*

Nora? *"Nora"* means a burrow, a hole in the ground an animal lives in—a dark, dank place. She was my sister. Played the piano incessantly. She took the bus or rode the bicycle a few times a week to see her piano teacher in the village unless he stopped by at our place. She always walked past me looking through me as if I wasn't there. Played with the two daughters of the school principal in the village and walked around with them holding hands as if afraid they'd lose each other.

*Your mother?*

She had huge blue eyes and chestnut hair cut short on the sides and in the back, exposing the nape of her neck. She was nearsighted and wore gold-framed *pince-nez* glasses we called *"cviker,"* from German "Zwicker." She tried to avoid wearing them, but still they left permanent tiny kidney-colored

7

Yuriy Tarnawsky

and –shaped marks on the bridge of her nose. She was often sick and would then move slowly, stopping frequently, as if not sure she could make it to where she was going. Wore beautiful clothes, loose blouses or dresses with skirts just below the knee, golden or copper-colored silk stockings, and high-heeled shoes. When the weather was colder, she wore loose overcoats that she kept wrapped tightly around herself. In the winter—a long red-fox fur coat and a matching muff. She rarely went bareheaded outside and wore cloche hats pulled down low over her forehead which seemed to cast permanent black-circle shadows under her eyes. She spoke softly to servant girls in the kitchen and to everyone in general. Sometimes, when she wasn't teaching at school, she would go into Nora's room and play the piano—beautifully and softly, so that you could barely hear it. (Nora always banged away furiously at the keys.) I preferred to sit then on the floor by the door in the next room, leaning on the wall even when it was open, listening to her play. The music seemed more beautiful that way.

Being very health-conscious, she made Nora and me drink an infusion of bitter wormwood before each supper, to help our digestion, and in wintertime breathe the vapor of potassium hypomanganate by making us lean over a basin filled with boiling water with our heads covered with a thick towel, to prevent us from getting a cold. I liked both, the first one because it tasted bad and I had to prove to myself that I could do it, and the second because the basin seemed a beautiful round lake of purple water over which I glided way up in the

8

sky like a hawk on its silent wings. Nora hated the first, but I don't know how she felt about the second. She never talked about it.

There were many photographs of mother before she married father—in the winter, in a skiing outfit and on skis with a bunch of friends on a snow-covered mountain slope, fencing, doing gymnastics in a strange outfit, swimming, some duplicates, often in different tints—blue, green, pink, brown, black.

*And your father?*

You could tell he was a soldier even when he wore civilian clothes. His back was always straight as if he was sitting on a horse no matter what he was doing. He even walked like that except when walking around the table at night thinking his thoughts. Then he looked like everyone else. There was a permanent halo of silver-gray light around him—his steel-gray eyes, silver temples, smooth-shaven vertical cheeks, lips tightly pressed together like a steel lock, and the well-tailored gray suits. But his lips and breath were warm as he kissed me to sleep at night. And so was his strong hand that held mine as we walked outside.

But he looked best in his mustard-colored, tight-fitting officer's uniform with the high four-cornered cap on his head which had a shiny black visor with a metal rim around its edge, the silver insignia on his collar like a lightning flash caught and forced to remain there still forever, the wide brown belt with its brass buckle around his waist, a matching pistol holster with the pistol in it on the side, and the tall shiny black boots. Most fascinating was the pistol which was black but shone as if made from silver, with a mysterious red dot in one spot, which I was sometimes permitted to look at and even touch, but never to take in my hands.

Each summer he would go away for a couple of weeks for military training, and even though I missed him then, I also liked to think about what he was doing, ordering the troops to do this and that while sitting high up on his horse. When he came back, I would ask him to describe what he had been doing and it was like I'd been there myself.

*There was a bench by the building?*

There was a park bench by the side of the building next to the drive that curved around to the manor house. It was made of thin wooden slats painted white that neatly curved down up front to make your legs feel comfortable and also high up in the back where you leaned.

*And a photograph of you on the bench?*

There was a photograph of me being held by my mother as she is sitting on the bench, with Nora on her left and father behind them, standing up. It must have been taken either in early spring or late fall because all of us are warmly dressed, although not as you would dress in winter. And there is no snow on the ground. Actually, it must have been in early spring of the year after I was born because I look more than just a few weeks old which would have been if it was in the fall of the preceding year but definitely not more than a year. I have a white knit cap on my head tied under my chin and a matching warm knit baby suit with feet. Nora has also a knit cap on her head, but it's gray and hugs her head tightly and has two flaps that go down over her ears. She's wearing a light-colored overcoat and dark thick stockings we called *"rajtuzy,"* that is tights. Mother is wearing a dark overcoat and a gray cloche hat and father a gray wide-lapelled overcoat and has a gray fedora hat on his head.

*Just one picture?*

There were a few of them, not different color tints like those of mother but all the same black and white except with parts of them cut off with scissors. I remember now, there was actually another woman sitting on the bench a little away from mother, on her right, and in the picture I described above she has been cut off. She looks young, younger than mother, and is also wearing a gray overcoat and has a little round black hat on her head. And father isn't standing behind mother and Nora but in the gap between mother and the woman.

And then there was still another picture with both the woman and father cut off as well as a second uncut version.

Yuriy Tarnawsky

*Who was the woman?*

I think it was probably *panna*—miss—Adela. She looked different in the picture than I remember what she looked like, but that may be because she was a few years younger then.

*Who was Adela?*

I'm not sure. She was someone father worked with sometimes but I don't know if she was a relative of the hrabia or an employee. I think she stayed sometimes at the manor house but lived someplace else most of the time.

She liked me a lot and would pat me on the head all the time and sometimes give me a kiss—on top of my head or on my eyes. She said I had beautiful eyes.

*Who cut up the pictures?*

I have no idea. It may have been Nora, who wanted to have a picture of father by himself, so she cut off that side by mistake in two of the pictures and then cut off the picture of father in one of them to keep, or if it wasn't Nora then it would have been most likely mother, wanting to have a picture of only the four and then the three of us.

But it was most likely Nora who'd done it for a reason only she herself knew. She was mysterious in many ways.

# 2

_____

*Your father and panna Adela drove away in a car?*

It was early in the morning and I was playing among the blackcurrant bushes along the front wall of our home, drugged by their heavy, heady smell, as always pretending to be a giant in a tiny miniature world, while hearing through the open window the loud voices of father and mother arguing about something on the background of Nora furiously playing the piano in her room.

Then a big cream-colored car with its top down and panna Adela behind the steering wheel drove up along the drive and stopped in front of the door. It had shiny chrome-coated wire wheels and light brown leather seats that contrasted beautifully with the creamy color of the car. Its doors opened front to back rather than the usual back to front and had shiny metal handles.

As soon as the car arrived, the argument inside stopped and father came rushing out the door, ran up to the car, opened it, got inside, and sat down in the front passenger seat. He wore a light gray suit and shiny black shoes and his head was bare. Panna Adela was in a flowery dress and her head was tied in a white silk scarf.

I jumped out of the bushes and running up to the car asked father where he was going. His face brightened up as he saw me and he said he and panna Adela had to go to the city on a business matter and would be back later that afternoon.

Panna Adela smiled at me, they both waved their hands in my direction, and the car drove off, looping around the drive and heading toward the exit from the estate.

I noticed then that inside the house it was now all quiet. Nora's playing had stopped.

*Your mother and Nora then came out?*

Moments later mother and Nora walked out the door and, without paying attention to me, as if they didn't see me, walked off quickly along a path that led toward the park. They both wore light summer dresses. Nora walked on mother's right and after a few steps she wrapped her arm around mother's, squeezed herself up to her, and walking in this fashion they disappeared among the trees.

*The little carriage drove up?*

I didn't feel like playing inside the bushes anymore and didn't know what to do. But just then Adek and Bodek drove up in the little two-wheeled carriage pulled by the pony. They stopped and asked me if I wanted to come along.

I gladly agreed, climbed into the carriage, and squeezed myself in between the two of them. Bodek sat on the left, holding the reins, and Adek on the right. We drove off to the right along one of the paths, Bodek snapped the reins for the pony to run faster, and it went galloping on its short legs down the smooth sand-packed path.

Adek had his beautiful Flobert rifle with him with a shiny black barrel and a light brown, almost yellow polished wooden stock and would aim it high up in the trees as if shooting at birds but would only call out, "Paff, paff, paff!"

When we were driving past one of the statues he would aim the gun at it and again call out, "Paff, paff, paff!"

As the carriage would slow down from time to time, I was afraid of falling overhead first and held on to Adek by wrapping my arms around his waist.

He looked at me, laughing, and asked if I was afraid to die.

I had a vague idea of what that meant but wasn't quite sure and asked him to explain.

He said it was to go up there, and pointed to the tops of the trees.

I asked if it was where the birds were who sang all the time.

He laughed and said, no, that it was higher, way up in the sky... in heaven.

But was it nice up there too? I asked. Like where the birds lived?

He said, yes, that it was nice, and even nicer.... nicer than anyplace on earth.

I said then that, yes, I wouldn't mind dying but after a while, considering the implications, added that I would do it as long as I was able to come down when I wanted, to see my parents and everyone else.

Both of the boys then laughed, saying, yes, that that would be nice, that they wouldn't mind dying then either. Who wouldn't want to go to heaven if he could come down to earth whenever he wished?

# 3

———

*Sunday dinners?*

We always had dinner right after coming home from the morning church service on Sundays.

I loved soups, in particular chicken broth with noodles, which was called *"rosil,"* tomato and rice soup, and sorrel soup with rice and hardboiled eggs.

The noodles were made from thin sheets of dough rolled into rolls which were sliced up into fine strips with a knife. These were fluffed up, dusted with flour, and left to dry a little on a cloth. They were boiled separately in water before being served with the flavorful broth. Putting a spoonful of them in your mouth seemed like swallowing a mouthful of hot and salty seltzer water, which I thought was nice.

Tomato soup was made with rice cooking together with the tomatoes, and had lots of sour cream added to it when it had cooled off, making it the color of pale coral. The bland taste of the sour cream and the glutinous rice toned down the harsh flavor of the tomatoes, making the combination just barely tart.

The dark sorrel leaves floating in the clear broth gave the latter a delicate acidic taste. Rice was cooked separately and added before serving. A hardboiled egg was sliced lengthwise in two and put in the plate after that, as was a spoonful or two of sour cream. The nearly flavorless rice, the bland egg white, and the crumbly dry egg yolk which dissolved readily in the broth counterbalanced the tangy liquid.

The main course was frequently meat patties fried in lard or butter called *"šnycli*—schnitzels—which were served with mashed potatoes and creamed beets or thinly sliced cucumbers with vinegar or dill and sour cream, called for some reason *"mizerja,"*—misery—roast chicken served with mashed potatoes and puree of carrots or beets, or beef pot-roast served with boiled potatoes and horseradish and sour cream sauce.

Dessert was typically a compote of available fruit, a thin cake of crumbly butter pastry with a layer of preserve in the middle called *"pljacok,"* cut up into small rhomboids or squares, and for special occasions a walnut, hazelnut, or poppy seed torte with a thick layer of sugared butter in the middle.

*Father and mother dancing?*

Sometimes after the Sunday dinner, when the table had been cleared off and the maids were doing the dishes in the kitchen, father and mother would dance in the open space around the table, between it and the wardrobe and windows.

We had a radio which was powered by a big battery we called *"akumuljator,"* consisting of a glass box and a bunch of metal panels joined together that went down in it, into which you had to pour acid from time to time to keep it going. I liked the way the acid smelled and would have liked to taste it but was told to stay away from it as it could harm me, burning my mouth and skin, and possibly even blinding me. That terrified me and I heeded the warning and never gave in to my temptation.

The radio was housed in a big square box made of a shiny hard black material, with a narrow glass window across it that had a turn knob on each side, one of which moved a thin red vertical line back and forth across the window and the other one adjusted the volume. Strange beautiful sounds would come out of the box as you turned the first knob, as if some exotic bird lived inside the box and moving the line made it sing its song. The song was different from those of the birds that lived in the park trees in an unusual way, however, as if the bird was mad.

The window was lit and there seemed to be a magical world inside the box where tiny people, even smaller than ants lived, speaking, singing, and playing music, and I dreamed about getting inside it to spend some time among them before returning back to the one I lived in.

We also had a record player that consisted of a flat gray rectangular box with a handle, looking like a small suitcase, which had a crank on one of its sides. You opened the top, turned the crank until you couldn't do it any longer, put the record through a spindle sticking up onto a circle that was able to rotate, pushed a lever which made the circle spin, lowered with your fingers a shiny metal arm with a thick sharp needle on the end onto the record, and once again beautiful music would fill the air. Spinning, the record looked like a lake similar to the washbasin with potassium hypomanganate dissolved it, except this one black and seen from a very tall far away mountain instead of up in the air, with music under its shimmering surface, which the needle was making come out.

The dancing would be done to the sounds of either the record player or the radio playing, with the light streaming in through the windows caught like cobwebs on the white floor-length curtains, and Nora and I would sit still at the table or on the sofa watching father and mother dance, spellbound by the ease with which they glided across the shiny parquet floor. Tall and slender in his gray suit, his back as always straight and his face calm, father would keep his left arm raised high, holding mother's right hand in his while supporting her with his right hand on the back of her waist, spinning her around and guiding along. Leaning back, her curly hair swaying, mouth open, eyes smiling, and the loose knee-length skirt swirling around her thighs, mother looked years younger than she was in reality, almost as she did in her pictures in school. Their feet in the shiny, well-polished shoes—father's pointed, flat, mother's rounded, with thick high heels—traced out complex incomprehensible patterns on the background of the floor, now close together, almost touching, now far away from each other, as if capable of sensing their partner's location through some magical means.

Had anybody asked me then what I would have liked for my life to be I would have answered that it was to sit still and look on like this forever.

# 4

_____

*Under rhododendron bushes?*

Under the rhododendron bushes along the right wing of the manor house. They got more sunlight there and were thicker and taller than on the other side.

It was late in the morning, and I got tired of playing among the blackcurrant bushes next to our house and decided to run over there. When I got to the spot I usually played in I saw something black and white stirring among the branches and thought at first it was some kind of an animal—a black and white dog or something—but then realized it was a girl. She looked a few years older than me, had long blond braids, and wore a black dress trimmed with white and with a wide white collar. I had never seen her before and was too shy to come up to her or say something, but didn't want to run away and stood still, watching what she was doing.

*Karolina?*

It was Karolina. She was Adek's and Bodek's cousin, and she had come to spend part of the summer with them.

*You played with her?*

She saw me and told me to climb into the bushes so that she could show me something.

I gladly did that and kneeled down on the soft ground beside her.

Look, she said, pointing to the bare branches twisting their way up from the ground, these are roads and paths for people to walk along.  There are these little people, the size of ants, who live in tiny villages down here on the ground, tilling the soil and raising all sorts of food, which they then carry up these roads and paths to the top to sell them at the market.

Their time is different than ours. It's still night there and they are sleeping, but when it gets lighter they get up and some of them go to work in the fields and others go to markets.  They carry what they've raised and sell it there and bring back the money home and things they've bought, such as candy and toys for children, pots and pans, knives, spoons, and forks, combs and mirrors, necklaces for girls, and things like that, which they don't make themselves.

She traced the paths along the branches as she told me how these people climbed and I followed her with interest.

Then we began pretending that it had gotten light in the little peoples' world and she would tell me what she saw, and I did the same, and we played like that until lunch time.

Yuriy Tarnawsky

We played in this fashion every day from then on, among the rhododendrons, the blackcurrant bushes in front of the building where I lived and next to the manor farm buildings, as well as among the bushes and trees in the park, and she invited me into the manor house to see her room, and I had tea and cake with her a few times, and it went on like this all summer.

*Peeing?*

Once, as we were playing under the rhododendrons, I noticed she was no longer next to me, and as I looked around, I saw she was squatting down a few feet behind me peeing, having lowered down her panties.

I didn't know what girls looked like down there and found what I saw fascinating and couldn't take my eyes off her.

Noticing that, she told me I could come up closer and look, which I did. She let me do it for a while even after she had stopped peeing, but then asked me to show her how I peed.

Without hesitation, I opened my shorts and tried peeing but for some reason couldn't. She had pulled up her panties by then and was kneeling next to me and reached out with her hands and touched my thing.

It was hard and she said it looked like an acorn and asked me if it was broken because it was so hard and wouldn't pee.

I said that there was nothing wrong with it, that it got hard like that sometimes, but would soon get soft again, and that it was only that for some reason I couldn't pee. I was sure I would be able to do it later.

She was satisfied with my answer and we went back to playing where we'd left off as if nothing had happened.

We never talked about this afterwards as if we'd erased it from our memories, and continued playing as before until she went away at the end of the summer.

*She came back the next summer?*

She came back the next summer and one more after that but we never played like we did the first year again. She had grown up and was pretending to be a young lady, dressing up in fancy clothes and fixing up her hair, and sometimes would paint her face with the hrabina's rouge and put lipstick on her lips if she was able to get to them, and it was as if we'd never been playmates.

# 5

------

*Under the stars?*

For a while I slept at night outside, trying to toughen myself up. My father had told me how he used to do it when he was little, to steel himself for whatever life might bring him, so I wanted to do it too. Mother was dead set against it but father said it'd do me good and I was permitted to do it.

I thought I'd do it on the ground next to our house but was told it was too dangerous because some animal could come along and bite me, and since the building we lived in had just one floor and thus no balcony it was arranged for me to sleep on the terrace at the manor house. I had a thin little pallet that I kept at home rolled up and I would take it with me, spread it out on the bench that was there, wrap myself up in a blanket, and sleep like that.

It was uncomfortable to sleep on a hard surface and without a pillow at first but gradually I got used to it and in the end began to enjoy it like something pleasurable. Every second of discomfort I felt seemed a drop of an antidote to the pain that I would have to endure in the future. If I persisted, there'd be nothing I wouldn't be able to withstand when it finally came. It was in the fall and nights were getting cold but the sky was clear and full of stars and I couldn't tear my eyes away from it, looking out from under the blanket, until I fell asleep unaware of doing it, soaked to the full with its beauty and vastness like a piece of blotting paper that'd absorbed all the liquid that'd been spilled on it.

Sometimes I would wake up in the middle of the night and in the beginning would feel lonely and homesick for my bed and the shelter of my parents' bedroom and would be overcome then with an urge to gather up my things and run with tears in my eyes for the love and comfort I would find there, but each time was able to stop myself and remained on the bench. I would face much more difficult things in the future and how would I be able to withstand them if I couldn't endure this little bout of loneliness I was experiencing? I had to be strong and not give in to my weakness. Calmed down, I would fall asleep and would wake up in the morning proud of having been strong at night.

*It rained?*

One night it rained and I woke up cold and wet, feeling instinctively that I shouldn't be staying on, but didn't know how to get back home. The doors in the manor house were all locked and how was I going to open them? I couldn't wake people up. What would they think of me? I thought of hiding in the gallery but there was no bench there and I didn't want to sleep on the cold stone floor. I rolled up into as tight a ball as possible, hid under the blanket, and lay shivering, not knowing what to do. Soon thereafter, though, I heard mother's frantic screaming down below under the balustrade, urging me to wake up. She'd been woken up by the rain and ran over to get me.

Somehow, they got me home, I was dried off, dressed in fresh bed clothes, given warm milk to drink, and put to bed, which felt better than ever before.

*You got sick?*

I was fine next day but at night got the shivers, was put to bed, and ran a high fever. They called the doctor in the morning, he came over, and it turned out I had pneumonia.

I was sick for more than a month, running high temperature and being drenched with sweat so that my clothes and sheets had to be changed, and had horrible nightmares of my tongue being a vast plain covered with big sharp stone boulders whose terrible sharpness and hardness I tasted, which I remember to this day, along which I had to travel, running into the boulders all the time and hurting myself on their sharp edges, and was fed clear chicken broth and lemonade, and had my chest rubbed with badger fat, and was cupped on my back, and had leeches stuck on my body which fell off lazily by themselves after having gotten fat from gorging themselves on my blood which I was too weak to brush off, and had to teach myself to walk all over again when I got better, holding on to chairs and tables, and slipping on the hard wooden floor in my hard-heeled and hard-soled shoes.

It took months for me to get well. Mother said I'd gotten sick because of my having been chilled but father argued that you didn't get pneumonia from getting chilled but from being infected with a bacillus but admitted that I could have gotten sick because my resistance to infection had been weakened because of my having gotten cold. It was agreed, though, that it was too risky for me to sleep outside again and I never went back to it, having myself lost taste for it anyway.

# 6

_____

*In closed spaces?*

The wardrobe, among clothes, especially if you closed the door, was fine to hide in but under the beds was better. My bed was a little high but my parents' was perfect—it was low and you lived in a small world there, different from the real one. I would dream up all sorts of stories while hiding under it and wanted to tell them to other people. But if there was no one to listen to me, it was fine too. I would curl into a ball, close my eyes, and let things happen as they wanted. It was like living a different life. Being out in the open interfered with my thinking but being hemmed in made me free.

The trouble was, though, that it was hard for people to climb in there with me. I convinced Nora to go in with me a few times until she started to complain that I wasn't leaving her alone. Mother got into the wardrobe with me once or twice but she couldn't get in under their bed. And father was too busy for such things.

*What were the stories like?*

It was mostly about little people—gnomes. For some reason I loved that the most. They were closer in size to me and lived in a world different from the real one, which was most important. In this world things happened in an uninteresting way but in the other one you could do anything you wanted.

I would dream up about them living in the park or in the bushes around buildings, as we did with the real tiny people with Karolina, but I especially loved the story I made up about these four gnomes that lived on a magic island that changed its shape all the time, far away in an ocean.

They were called Romo, Oro, Momo, and Moro, and they were running into trouble all the time. They were small like all gnomes but had big feet, which sometimes got in their way. They loved dancing together and because their feet were so big would step on each other's toes all the time and yell, "Stop it!" and "Stop it!" and slap each other, and get into a real fight. They would dig a hole in the ground sometimes and travel to a still different world, turned upside down, where everything was pink, or blue, or purple.

But most of their time was spent fighting a huge black dragon called Black Tooth. He fed on coal and would fly to a coalmine to gorge himself on coal or to a market to buy some and would come back with huge sacks filled with it, carrying them under each of his sixteen legs, so as to eat later. He lived in a cave which had a door that he would lock with a key he kept under a rock when he flew away, and the gnomes knew about it, and would get the key and unlock the door so that when he

31

came back, being very stupid, he would lock the door thinking he was opening it and then would tear off the door handle and curse about what happened.

He needed coal because there was a fire burning in his belly and when it went out he'd die and his dragon wife would have to open the door he had on the bottom, and shovel coal in there, and start a fire, to bring her husband back to life.

The gnomes had glass jars filled with time which, when you opened them, would stop everyone else from moving so that you could do whatever you wanted while the world around you stood still. When things got tough for them as they fought Black Tooth, they'd open their jars and then open the door in his belly, and shovel out the burning coal, and when they closed the jar, Black Tooth was dead and his wife had to build a fire in his belly once again.

The gnomes had also a little mushroom friend called Ero who was very brave. He fought with them against Black Tooth and would stick his sharp spear into his belly to distract him from fighting. The trouble was that the gnomes had to do a lot of thinking how to fight Black Tooth and Ero had to be prevented from doing it because his cap, which was his head, would heat up and he was in danger of cooking himself. So, when the gnomes were thinking and saw steam rising out of Ero's cap, they knew he was in trouble and they would pour water on him, and push him around, and so on, so that he wouldn't think, and bring him back to life.

*You had a brother?*

At one point I went through a period of pretending that I had a brother who lived beyond the ocean and was very poor because he lived alone and didn't have anybody to take care of him. He was the same age as me, so he would have been my twin, although I never thought of him as such. He was just my brother whom I felt great love for and who needed my help.

There was a little brook flowing through the park close to our home, so I started sending him things by putting them on pieces of board I would find around the farm buildings in the estate, or flat pieces of wood, or other things that floated such as tin cans and metal bowls. The brook would carry them to a big river, which would carry them to the sea, which would finally bring them to him.

At first, I sent him some of my favorite toys and even convinced Nora to send some of hers too, although she lost interest in it after a couple of tries and refused to participate any more. But it was getting cold, and I started sending him some of my clothes, and then food, sometimes what I was having myself, for instance for breakfast, because I usually ate it alone.

It was noticed then that some dishes and flatware were missing and also my warm clothes, and that I was disappearing somewhere with my breakfast from time to time, and Nora

Yuriy Tarnawsky

told my parents about the brother I had dreamed up and what I had been doing, and so I was forced to stop doing this although I went on believing in my brother's existence for a while.

*A sword?*

I had a beautiful little sword that was given to me for one of my birthdays and it was another aid for my stories.

I would pretend galloping on a horse while cutting off heads of enemy soldiers as I ran through a clearing in the park, cutting off tops of flowers while emitting blood-curdling screams at the top of my voice.

I wanted to do it while riding the pony but was forbidden because it was feared I would fall down and hurt myself.

*Nora's doll?*

I got into real trouble with Nora's doll. It was the biggest one she had and her favorite, made from *kavčuk*—hard rubber—and was hollow inside.

I always wanted to know what it was like on the inside and one day while practicing my swordsmanship in the living room, when no one was around, I decided to cut off the doll's head with the sword and take a peek.


34

The doll sat on Nora's bed propped up by a pillow. I set it up so that its head was sticking up and swung with the sword at its neck. It did some damage to the doll but didn't sever the head. The doll had toppled over and lay on its side and in an attack of frenzy I couldn't control I began hacking away with the sword at its neck until the head came off.

*What was it like inside?*

It was nothing special on the inside—just hollow. It looked moist, though, which intrigued me, and so I rubbed my finger on the inside of the head and tasted it and found it was salty like sweat. There was also a little white cube like a lump of sugar made of some light material glued to the back of the head on the inside. I tried to figure out what it was for but couldn't, yet didn't want to ask anyone, afraid of attracting attention to what I'd done as if believing it wouldn't be noticed.

It was noticed, of course, and there was little doubt who had done it, and I confessed without hesitation I did it, when asked.

*You were punished?*

Nora went hysterical when she saw what I had done, screaming and crying, and locked herself up in the room, and wouldn't come out all evening, and didn't talk to me for days. I don't think she ever forgave me.

Mother wanted me to be spanked but father said that spanking didn't correct bad behavior but promoted it by showing that violence was acceptable. Instead, I was to stand in the corner when everyone was having supper and go to bed hungry for three days.

I enjoyed this punishment however and would willingly have gone on with it longer. I stood straight as a rod, staring at the blank wall before me, hearing the clinking of spoons and knives and forks hitting the china behind my back while hunger chafed on my stomach, feeling myself grow readier by the second to face those bad things life would one day throw at me.

The second night mother wanted to give me some food as I was going to bed in secret, without father's knowing, but tempted though I was to accept her offer, I firmly refused it and fell asleep even happier than I was as I stood facing the wall. Had I accepted her offer it would have spoiled all I'd accomplished.

The third night she left me alone.

# 7

_____

*Your grandmother?*

Every summer we would go to stay for a few weeks with my grandmother who lived far away in the mountains. We would take one train for a short distance first and then change to another, in which we traveled for hours. It took almost the whole day to get there.

I liked the second part of the trip the most. We would usually be alone in the compartment and I would sit next to the open window, facing in the direction we traveled, the inrushing air like a cold pillow pressed tight against my face, making it hard for me to breathe. It was mixed with the smoke coming out of the engine and smelled of hardboiled eggs, like those we consumed with sandwiches mother had prepared and brought along in a big basket, which I liked.

I liked even more to stick my head out the window and then be really smothered by the air so that I would gasp but would be told not to do it because of the danger of a spark in the smoke getting into my eye and blinding me. Afraid as I was of that, I couldn't resist the temptation of leaning out the window time and time again however, especially on the curves, because then I could see the whole train from the engine up front to the last car at the end. They both looked surprisingly small, almost like toys, and the train shorter than I had thought it was, which I found nice.

Sometimes father would have enough of my behavior however and would angrily close the window, raising it up with a leather strap that stuck out through a gap in the sill.

The air would get progressively colder and fresher as we got higher into the mountains. Everybody liked that, and the window would be lowered again if it had been raised, and I would behave so that it wouldn't be closed again.

There was a tunnel we had to go through before arriving at our destination, and the compartment would get all dark when we went in it, the air would reek of smoke, and the clamor the train made, now reverberating off the stone walls, got so loud you couldn't hear anything else.

This went on for a long time so that it seemed it would never end but then, suddenly, everything was bright again, the air smelled fresh, the clamor was gone, and you could hear the rhythmic clicking the wheels of the train were making as they rolled along the rails. The town lay spread out in front of us below the high viaduct and the train proceeded at a slow pace along it before arriving at the station on the other side.

It had white stucco walls and a red-tiled roof and there were flowerpots suspended from its eaves with red flowers in them that looked like flames.

The *peron*—platform—around it was paved with tiles divided into little squares, which made it look like a chocolate bar, and walking along it your feet made sharp clicking noises like a chocolate bar breaking, and I always felt as though I was walking along a huge chocolate bar with its silver paper stripped off when we came to stay with my grandmother and was especially looking forward to it.

*She waited for you?*

Grandmother always waited for us in front of the station in a fiacre, its hood folded down in the back, all in black, her head tied in a shawl and wearing a floor-length dress, her hands on the ivory handle of a cane she carried outside.

She would kiss me when I got inside the fiacre beside her and would press into my hand a chocolate bar such as I imagined as I walked down the peron, which she produced from somewhere among the folds of her dress and which she knew I expected, our luggage would be put in the trunk in the back, my parents and Nora would squeeze themselves into the front and back seats which faced each other, the driver would get up on his high seat, crack his whip, and the fiacre would roll off into town.

Yuriy Tarnawsky

The street was paved with cobblestones, and the noise the horse's hoofs made on it made me think again of the sound a chocolate bar makes when you break it, and I was looking forward to hearing the sound the one grandmother gave me would make as I was breaking it once we got to her place and ate what she'd prepared for us. You shouldn't have sweets before a meal and not let your stomach run your life.

*You ate what?*

Home-baked sour-dough rye bread, shiny and with the imprint of a cabbage leaf on top of the loaf, with freshly churned butter, and curds with sour cream and radishes and scallions and dill, and fresh buttermilk to drink along with it, and sorrel soup with rice and sour cream and sliced hard-boiled egg in it like mother used to make, and stewed rabbit in sour cream sauce with mashed potatoes and puréed beets, and white cheese patties sautéed in butter, served with cherry and currant preserves, and honey bread, and wild strawberries, and raspberries, and blueberries, served with sugar and cream, and mint tea with honey, and local mineral water with raspberry syrup or without it to finish off.

*You went to sleep?*

The lightly starched and carefully ironed linen gently caressed my skin as I crawled in between the sheets and instantly slid off into sleep as if head first along a slippery, steeply inclined board, accompanied by the sweet smell of apples that were used to scent it in the chest in which it was kept.

*A singing gate?*

There was a flower garden in front of the house separated from the street by an iron fence. The gate in it made a sound like a bird chirping discreetly a few times and then falling silent as you opened or closed it.

*Flowers in the garden?*

Along the fence grew red climbing roses. A wide yellow brick path running from the gate to the front door cut the garden in two and went around each of the two rectangles, which took up the rest of the garden and were edged with the same kind of bricks, stood up vertically at an angle. In the center of each, there was a large circle with white peonies along the edge in one of them and pink ones in the other, and tall flaming red dahlias in the middle. A thick carpet of mountain pinks filled in the rest of each rectangle. They gave off a sweet, heady smell when it got dark, which persisted until dawn. It was so strong it sometimes woke me up in the middle of the night.

*A singing water pump?*

There was a water pump in the vegetable garden in the back of the house. It made a sound like a bird singing as you pumped it, going on and on, never ready to stop. I had to fight sometimes to move the handle as we were filling the bucket because I liked to be the one who made it sing.

Yuriy Tarnawsky

*The water?*

The water flowing out of the spigot into the bucket felt like a man's muscular arm.  The one in the bucket smelled like a sheaf of cold flowers.

*The garden in the back?*

A huge apple tree grew in one corner of the garden in the back, which sunlight barely penetrated.  It was always half-dark among its branches as during a moonlit night. The apples were small and red, and seemed to hop around on the branches like birds as you tried to pick them.  You could hear them falling into grass at night like flutes making long sad sounds which I likewise liked.

There were also red and yellow currant bushes growing in it with the berries like tiny suns, red or yellow, bunched up in tight constellations, gooseberries, their yellow-green insides murky like stagnant water, strawberries growing in neat rows that exploded in your mouth with flavor as you bit into them, threatening to puncture through your palate, carrots growing in even neater rows, sweet, as if dipped in sugar as you chewed on them after washing them off under the pump, as well as cabbage, kohlrabi, and sweet peas climbing nimbly along tall espaliers, the peas inside the pods like drops of green sugar water and the pods sweet too after you pulled the clear membrane off them.

*You went swimming?*

Sometimes mother would prepare food for the whole day which she would put in the basket she had brought along on the train, and we would hire a fiacre to take us to a big river a few kilometers outside of town and pick us up later. There were hardly any people ever on it, but wide flat pebble beaches among tall osier bushes, and we would spread out our blanket and towels on the one we liked and sun ourselves or bathe. The river was shallow with only occasional deep spots, and mother would swim there while I and Nora splashed around close to the bank. Her movements were smooth and silent as if she were a puddle of oil on the surface of water which was changing its shape all the time.

Father would usually stay on the blanket, reading a newspaper or playing chess by himself.

*And picnicking?*

Mother would prepare food once again, and we would go into the hills outside of town and picnic on top of one in the middle of a field in tall grass or on the edge of woods, where it was short. Usually there'd be just the four of us, but occasionally some friends of my parents would come along. They had two girls about Nora's age, and she would play with them while I played alone or listened to my parents and the other two adults talking. Father would sometimes play chess with the man if he was there, otherwise he would play by himself while I watched him make the moves and would ask questions.

Yuriy Tarnawsky

*Mushroom and berry picking?*

The woods were cool and smelled of resin, and the ground in them was slippery from pine needles that covered it like short-clipped hair so that you would slip on them and fall down if you weren't careful, and the mushrooms bulged out from under the soil like shy little animals afraid or unable to break through, or would stand strong and proud as if daring anyone to pick them. The ones with little caps on top of a big fat stem shaped like a barrel, called  *"bili"*— white—were the best, especially when served in a sour cream sauce, but I also liked the little yellow ones called *"lysyčky"*—little foxes—and the blue or purple ones *called "holubinky"*—pigeon mushrooms,—or anything else we picked.

It was hot in the clearings in the strong sunlight, and insects hummed in them like a harp that'd been plucked and thrown in the grass but which wouldn't grow still, and wild strawberries grew in them in the grass like drops of sweet fragrant blood, and you searched with your fingers for raspberries and blackberries under the leaves on the long climbing vines where they hid and would find them soft and obedient, letting you pick them, not trying to get away. Blueberries grew on short curly bushes, and you picked them with a special wide wooden comb, running it through the leaves as if through hair.

*A circus?*

There were a few circuses I saw as we were visiting my grandmother, but I especially remember one with a family of

44

acrobats performing all sorts of things, ending with a still-standing figure composed of all of them. There was the father, the mother, two boys, a girl, and a little black and white dog with a curled-up tail.

With the exception of the dog, they were all dressed in black and white striped one-piece short-sleeved bathing suits. The father stood with his legs bent in the knees and spread wide on top of a big white board, balancing on a huge black iron ball, his arms stuck out to the sides, while the mother sat on his shoulders with her legs wrapped along his chest and under his armpits, her arms spread out like her husband's. The boys, who were bigger than the girl, stood on top of the father's thighs, leaning out while holding onto his hands, and the girl sat on her mother's shoulders the way the latter sat on her husband's, her arms spread out in similar fashion, the dog curled up neatly on top of her head. He got there by himself by climbing along the bodies of the people quickly and skillfully like a monkey.

The figure remained still for a long time, all members of the family with the exception of the father as well as the dog smiling. The expression on the face of the former was one of unbelievable strain—it was swollen dark red, almost black with blood, his lips were tightly shut, his cheeks and eyes bulged, and the muscles and veins under his skin rippled like snakes trying to get away. You could see it was getting harder and harder for him to go on, and just as it looked like he was going to collapse, there was the sound of a shot going off somewhere and the whole figure disintegrated in an instant, everyone jumping down to the floor and bowing, including the dog.

They were rewarded with a roar of approval and applause from the audience, and stood for a long time straightening up and bowing, the father breathing heavily, trying to catch his breath.

*A dwarf elephant?*

Another attraction in that circus was a little white dwarf elephant, the size of a St. Bernard dog. His master was a bald elderly gentleman with gold-rimmed glasses, and the elephant did all sorts of things for him, such as counting, by taping its foot, and spelling out names, by pointing with its trunk to a chart with the alphabet on it.

I was so excited about it that I couldn't go to sleep all night and wanted to see it again the next day. It was Monday, and the circus was leaving that day, so there was no chance of my attending the performance again, but, seeing how excited I was, mother took me to where the circus camped and we were permitted to go to the owner's wagon.

It was smaller than some of the other, but very beautiful, made of yellow varnished wood trimmed with brass and with a round green metal top with brass gutters around it. Mother knocked on the door, and when the owner heard about why we were there, we were permitted to go inside. The elephant was there, in a little closed off area at the back of the wagon, with two blue armchairs and a matching sofa in it. Its skin was actually a pale gray, rather than pure white, and where it creased, was blue, like marks left by a carbon copy as you run something sharp over it.

We sat on the sofa and the owner and the elephant in the armchairs, the latter somewhat awkwardly, supporting itself with one of its front legs and looking at me with interest with its small shiny red eyes of a wise old man. It counted off my age when I said how old I was by gently tapping its foot as on the stage, and spelled my name by pointing to the chart. Then we were served tea in little white and blue china cups which the elephant poured from a matching white and blue teapot holding it with its trunk.

It squeezed my hand feebly with its trunk again, as if bored, as we were saying good-bye, and followed us with its eyes as we were going out the door.

*More stories?*

Except for the dwarf elephant, I didn't like elephants because of their bare sagging behinds and them walking obediently in a circle while holding in their trunks the tail of the one before them, and made up stories about how they floated like clouds in the sky after blowing themselves up like balloons by sticking their trunks into their behinds. Those who couldn't do it themselves had to ask their friends to do it for them. And if they didn't have friends, they'd stay on the ground and turn into soft rocks.

Giraffes were a different matter. I saw them in a zoo in a city close to where we lived, as well as in pictures, and was impressed by their incredibly long graceful necks. I told stories of some of them being so tall that their heads were up above the clouds and they lived on rain- and snow flowers which grew on top of the latter. When the weather was sunny, they grew hungry and had to find a tall steep mountain to graze on the side of it.

Their heads were so high up in the sky that they needed glasses to see what was happening on the ground. To be fitted for them, doctors needed very tall ladders to get to them, and only very brave ones would do it.

# 8

---

*The seashore?*

As I mentioned earlier, every summer father went away for a couple of weeks for military training, and one year it was decided that we should go for vacation on the seashore which was close by.

The day when he was finished, mother, Nora, and I took the train, and he was to meet us while we were passing through the city he was in. We took the same train as going to my grandmother's first, but then changed into a different one, with cars that had upholstered seats and compartments with walls covered with plush material; the seats in the train we took to grandmother's had wooden benches built similarly to the one in front of our house except of varnished yellow wood and walls of the same material.

The ride was even longer than the one to my grandmother's, and it was late in the afternoon when we arrived in the city where father was to meet us. I ran out into the corridor to watch for him through the open window. I kept looking for him among the people thronging on the platform, but he was nowhere to be seen. The crowd was getting thinner and thinner, and I was beginning to worry he wasn't coming, but then I noticed him way in the distance standing and talking to panna Adela. I was going to shout to him, although he probably wouldn't have heard me, but then they said good-bye to each other, panna Adela walked off in one direction and he in the opposite one, toward me. I was going to mention what I saw to mother but decided against it. I was sure she wouldn't have liked it. She stood next to me and, although she wore her glasses, I suspected she didn't see them. She saw poorly even with her glasses on. Nora was with us to but had been looking the other way.

He was wearing civilian clothes, carried a big suitcase in his hand, and was searching with his eyes for car numbers with a serious expression on his face. I did call out to him now, he saw me, his face brightened up, and he speeded up and walked toward the car we were in.

Soon he was in the corridor, embraced and kissed us all, we filed back into the compartment, and resumed our ride.

*A house on the shore?*

We had rented a room in a house on the edge of town, among dunes, close to the water. It was almost dark when we arrived at our station, and we took a carriage to where we were to stay.

Our room was on the second floor and you could see a strip of something light stirring in the distance above the dark tops of the dunes.  It was the sea.

A strong breeze, smelling of iodine, the kind you put on a wound when you cut yourself, blew from it, pushing the curtain on the window in my face as I would brush it aside over and over again, trying to look out.

I wanted to run right away to the sea to see it but was told it was too late.  We would see it together in the morning.

After a small meal in the dining room downstairs we went back to our room and then to bed.  I lay listening to the sound the sea was making like that of a tree rustling in the wind for a brief instant and then stopping, rustling for an brief instant and then stopping again, before, as always unaware of doing it, falling asleep.

*How was the sea?*

It was still and flat the next morning, and didn't make the kind of sound it made when we arrived.  The waves were small and they seemed to break on the sand absentmindedly like movements people make with their fingers without being aware of them, when they are nervous.

It was vast, though, with the sun reflecting off its surface like off a huge board painted silver gray, and I couldn't stop looking at it.

Yuriy Tarnawsky

*Your brother?*

I had ceased dreaming about having a brother a long time before then, but seeing the sea brought the memory back to me.

I saw the straight line of the horizon and said to myself that my brother stood there on the other shore thinking of me as I was of him.  But the direction I was looking was different from where I had imagined him before, and the idea no longer excited me as it did back then, and so I stopped thinking of him and never did again.

*You swam and did other things?*

I went swimming close to the shore, holding onto father's hand, although just for short stretches of time because the water was cold.  Father did it a lot, however, and Nora a little more than me.  But it was too cold for mother and she never went into the water.

We would lay out our blankets far away from other people, close to the dunes, where it was warmer, and would sun ourselves there and picnic.

Father would read newspapers and play chess by himself for hours at a time, and I would watch him and ask questions about what he was doing.

*Men with a wardrobe?*

One day two men came walking out of the dunes carrying a big wardrobe. They were shabbily dressed and unkempt, and looked like hobos.

They walked into the water, dropped the wardrobe into it, and started swimming alongside it, pushing it along, away from the shore. Everyone stood up and watched them for a long time, until you couldn't see them anymore.

People talked about it for days, and there were write-ups about it in the newspapers, but nobody knew who the men were, why they had done it, and what happened to them.

Mother thought they wanted to get to the country on the other shore, but father said it would have been crazy to try that because it was too far. They could have never made it. He said it was probably just a stunt made to confuse everyone. They were probably picked up later by a boat.

But I knew they were both wrong. The men just wanted to take the wardrobe with them into the sea. Why was it so hard to understand?

———

*The hrabina?*

I saw very little of her, and never out in the open. She was sick all the time and didn't go out, but always stayed indoors.

I would see her, tall and very thin, dressed in a long black dress or gown, walking slowly, holding onto walls and furniture, paying no attention to me as if she didn't see me as I was trying to get to where I was going, except once, when she stopped and in a voice as dark as herself asked me if I was the lieutenant's son, meaning my father's.

I was walking along the other side of the corridor, stopped myself, and, pressing against the wall, to feel safer, said in a guilty voice, as if I'd done something bad, that I was, but she said nothing in return and resumed her walking, and then I did too, slinking furtively along.

*Kids laughing?*

I don't know who these kids were and why they were there, or if they were there at all, and if they were why were there so many of them, and why were they running around laughing and I with them, but it was in the long dark corridor, so maybe I'm confusing the reflections of light on the floor with the sound of laughter. And also, maybe we, if those kids were there, or I alone, if they weren't, didn't run but walked, looking into rooms to see where her body lay.

Anyway, assuming the kids were there, we were going down the corridor and as we were passing a door, we would stop and open it, and go into the room, and look in, and then go out, and shut the door, and continue as before.

And in one of the rooms, I think the last one, we found her. She was stretched out on a table covered with a black satin cloth, herself dressed in black, the tips of her black patent leather shoes sticking out from under the edge of the dress, her hands crossed on her chest, as it looked, tied together with a rosary. Her face was yellow as wax, the cheeks hollow, the nose pinched, as if glued together, and the eyes huge and bulging under the eyelids.

We all stood quiet now, as if embarrassed at our earlier behavior, and then quietly, one by one, sneaked out of the room like smoke escaping, I believe in the end leaving the door open.

*You had a dream that night?*

That night I had a dream that all of us—father, mother, Nora, me, the hrabia, his sister Anna, Adek and Bodek, and some other people I don't remember are sitting around a huge long dining table covered with a white tablecloth and set for dinner with white porcelain dishes and silverware, with the hrabina stretched out in the middle like she was in reality, but dressed in white, with white flowers arranged all around her, also as in reality. But she is incredibly long, much longer than in reality, stretching the length of the huge table.

The hrabia is sitting at the head of the table, beyond the hrabina's head, Adek and Bodek on the other side on his left, the four of us across from them, father next to the hrabia on my left, and mother on my right, with Nora beyond her.

Everyone is eating and chatting, there's a clatter of silverware hitting porcelain and the sound of people's voices in the air, but my plate is still empty. My father notices this and decides to help me to some food. He sticks his right hand in among the flowers, looks for something with it, apparently finds it, and tries to tear it off for me. It seems to be part of something bigger. He's having a hard time doing this however, so he takes his right hand out, grabs his knife with it, sits up, sticks his left hand in where his right had been, and plunges the knife into the mound of flowers next to it. He struggles some more, twisting the knife back and forth, but finally brings something out, puts it on my plate, and sits down to continue what he's been doing. He has given me something that looks like a turkey drumstick. I pick it up with my hand, bite into it, and start eating.

As I do this, I glance at the hrabia and see him holding in his hands a big bone with a lot of meat on it, biting into it from time to time and chewing vigorously. He's smeared with grease ear to ear and there's a smile on his face—he seems to be having a great time.

But then I realize that it isn't grease that his face is smeared with but blood—his face is all red and the meat he's biting in isn't cooked but raw. I glance around the table and see that this is true of everyone—people aren't using their knives and forks as before but holding pieces of uncooked meat in their hands, are biting into them, and chewing what they'd bitten off, enjoying what they are doing. Adek and Bodek across the table from me are doing it, and so is father, and mother next to me, and Nora beyond her. She seems to be eating with a particular gusto—biting voraciously into what she is holding in her hands, sinking her teeth in deep, tearing off what she's bitten into, and chewing on it with relief on her face.

I realize then that my face is also smeared with something wet which must be blood and that what I'm holding in my hands is not a cooked turkey drumstick but a raw one and that the meat in my mouth is raw too. It's cold and stringy and has an insipid taste like a piece of rubber. I find it revolting and want to spit it out, but then feel my father nudge me on my left shoulder, urging me to swallow. I know I can't disobey him, so I swallow what I've bitten off, but at the same time retch and bring it up with everything else I had in my stomach. The disgust I feel is enormous, and I wake up screaming and sit straight up.

I felt extremely nauseous, and as I recalled the taste of the raw meat I felt in my dream, I retched and vomited all over my bed, crying and screaming at the top of my voice.

*And the funeral?*

It had rained during the night, the day was cold and gray, and everyone was dressed in overcoats, some of the people (the hrabia's family as well as other people, including my father and mother) wearing black bands on their sleeves and men carrying their hats in their hands. The faces of the women who wore hats were hidden behind black veils.

The procession consisted of a band marching up front, with all players dressed in black, playing something slow and dark on their brass instruments, followed by a black flat wagon with four fluted posts on the corners supporting a roof, covered with a black velvet cloth with a silver fringe hanging down. The coffin, which was black, trimmed with silver, stood in the middle of it on a raised platform covered with black velvet cloth. The wagon was pulled by four black horses with clumps of black plumes tied with silver bands on top of their heads, the driver, dressed in black and his head bare on the high seat behind them.

The hrabia, the two boys, his sister, and other members of his family who came for the occasion walked next, and the four of us behind them, I between my parents, holding their hands and Nora next to mother. We were followed by a huge throng of people—manor employees and friends of the family, with many of the inhabitants of the village as well as of some of the surrounding ones at the end.

When they had put the coffin in the grave and were throwing earth on it, I found myself next to Adek, and as you heard the hollow sound the lumps of earth were making, striking the lid of the coffin, he glanced at me, pointed with his finger up into the sky and then motioned with it down to earth, winking at the same time with an impish expression on his face, meaning his mother went up to heaven but would be coming down whenever she wanted.

# 10

---

*Pan Florian?*

*Pan*—mister—Florian was the postmaster in the village and a friend of my parents. He was tall and gangly, had a shiny bald head with a thin fringe of graying hair above the ears and the nape of the neck running around it, and pale blue eyes that looked like puddles of milky liquid. His joints constantly cracked very loudly so that it seemed he was breaking twigs when he walked or moved his arms, hands, or fingers.

He had a serious problem—from time to time big bumps, like giant boils the size of walnuts that wouldn't break through the skin, would appear on his forehead, nose, chin, under the eyes, and so on, and would completely change his appearance. They would stay there for a day or two and then disappear without a trace, as if they hadn't been there.

There was the ghost of a Babylonian general or vizier, named Bel-Rabim-Abilsil, who refused to enter the kingdom of the dead and wanted to inhabit pan Florian's body. For some reason he took a liking to it.

But pan Florian wouldn't agree to it, and fiercely fought against it. The ghost would come to him in his sleep at night, and they would have long arguments about it, and sometimes get into physical fights. The next day pan Florian would be pale and exhausted and often his face would change after that.

One morning he woke up with his bed all bloody and long gashes on his chest, belly, arms, and even face. He and the ghost had fought with Turkish scimitars all night long and inflicted wounds on each other.

But the gashes were shallow, more like scratches than cuts, and they healed in a couple of days, again without leaving a trace.

Other strange things would happen with pan Florian too. He would hold a box of matches in his hand, for instance, and the matches would fly up in the air, forming a neat arc and stay there for a few seconds, clinking like metal rods before falling to the ground. Similar things would happen to a deck of cards he held in his hand, for instance as he was about to deal from it—they would fly out of his fingers into the air, form a beautiful arc, hang there still for a while, and then fall to the ground like the matches.

He was a bachelor and lived alone. One night he was playing chess with the *kanonik*—village priest—when the door opened, a strange dog ran into the room, and as pan Florian yelled at it to go away, it turned into a pile of sand on the floor.

An old woman they'd never seen before then came in through the door with a broom, a dustpan, and a pail, swept up the sand and walked back out. When the maid came in the morning, there was still some sand left on the floor and she had to sweep it up.

He would come to dinner at our place from time to time and sometimes there'd be strange knocking heard coming from different places in the apartment, sometimes even the furniture, as well as the sound of footsteps and the clinking of a metal chain, and pan Florian would then say something angrily in a strange language, and the noises would stop. At times like this, father would sit with an expression of annoyance on his face, and mother and Nora pale and with their eyes bulging. I too would be scared and would feel chills running up my spine and hair on my head stand on end, but when the noises stopped, I wished for them to come back. Things like that were more exciting than regular life.

## 11

———

*Books?*

I loved books more than anything else in the world, even more than playing games and imagining things, and would incorporate what I found in them into my stories.

Every night before I went to sleep, whenever possible, father or mother would read to me sitting on the edge of their bed, with me beside them, following with my eyes and finger on the page what they were reading.

*You read too?*

I was too little to go to school but following them read and asking questions, I gradually started to be able to read myself a little. And since they couldn't read to me whenever I wanted, for instance during the day, I started to pick up the books myself and tried reading in them, again asking questions whenever necessary, so that in the end I was able to read everything.

*What were they?*

Yuriy Tarnawsky

At first, they were little children's books, then fairy tales such as "Hansel and Gretel," "Snow-White and the Seven Dwarfs," "Puss in the Boots," "The Ugly Duckling," and so on, and when I got older, stories of travel to distant lands, like Africa and America. I especially loved those about America with Indians in them, how they fought white people, scalping them when they killed them, frightened but unable to put the book away. But I liked reading about the good Indians among them too— those who were brave and noble, and imagined being an Indian myself. I learned that *"wigwam"* meant "house," and *"tomahawk"* — "hatchet," and *"moccasins"* — "shoes," and would say these words to myself, pretending to be an Indian.

But there were two books I liked the most.

The first one was called "Bad Boy Humphrey," about an English boy whom nobody liked but who was a kind person in reality. He was sullen, and didn't say much when among people, and didn't like to play with other kids but by himself or with animals, like dogs and horses, and when his father died and his mother remarried, he didn't get along with his stepfather and was sent away to a boarding school. He didn't get along with his fellow students and teachers there either, always standing up for something he believed in, and when one day he saw a teacher administering a brutal caning to a little underclassman boy for having done something, he intervened and, being very strong, knocked the teacher down, causing him to hit his head on the sharp edge of a stool and pass out.

He was going to be kicked out of the school the next day for what he'd done but prior to that was to spend the night up in a tower on top of the main hall as punishment. It was late in the year, cold, windy, and rainy, and there were no windows in the tower, and so he got wet and chilled, and was sick in the morning, running high temperature and delirious. It turned out that he got pneumonia and he died a few days later.

I felt great empathy for Humphrey, partly because I knew what pneumonia meant, and felt as if the story was about me, and asked mother if she would remarry and send me to a boarding school when father died. She looked at me in a strange way, as if holding something back, but then said that father wasn't going to die before her because he was younger than she and very healthy, and then added that if something like that did happen, if he was to be killed in the war for instance, she definitely would not remarry. She said she loved me and Nora very much and would always care for us, and embraced me, and then Nora, who had been listening to us talk and ran up to join us. Mother threw her arms around us and hugged us tightly, all three of us standing still as a stature for a long time. Nora was pressed close to me and I was surprised at how warm she felt—just like mother. We'd never stood so close to each other before.

The second book was called "Axel's Cave." It was about a Swedish boy named Axel, whose parents died all of a sudden and he was left alone. They were very rich and left him a lot of money, and he had a beautiful boat built for himself which he could sail alone, and he loaded it up with lots of food and other things, and sailed away on a journey around the world. He landed in Antarctica, and since it was summer there, with the sun shining all the time, he liked it a lot, and began exploring the place, and one day found a big cave in the side of a mountain, which was all fixed up as a home, with many rooms, and furniture, and everything else. It looked well-kept, and he thought someone lived there, but then he found the body of an old man lying in his bed, all shriveled up and light as a bundle of dry corn stalks. Next to the man, on the bedtable, was a note written in Swedish, stating that he had built the home himself and that he was leaving it for anyone who found it to use it as his own. He wrote it before dying.

It turned out that the cave was next to an underground hot water spring, with which the cave was heated, so that it was extremely comfortable for living year around. The man had devised clever ways of raising all sorts of food during the warm months, and catching fish, and preserving everything, and making fish oil which could be used for lighting and cooking fire, so that one could live there forever without needing to go for things someplace else, and described it all in a big notebook he left behind.

Axel was overjoyed with what he discovered. He buried the man's body in a grave he dug himself and decided to live in the cave from then on.

He found that one of the rooms had a big bulging window made of thick glass, which was covered with snow that had drifted over since the man's death. He cleared off the snow and saw that the room had been designed for watching stars at night. There was a comfortable armchair in the center of it with a telescope in front, and you could sit in the armchair and either watch the stars with a naked eye or through the telescope, whatever you preferred.

And so, he stayed there, and lived for a very long time, without ever seeing another person, not having a need for anyone, filling himself with the view of the starlit sky every night.

I loved the part of the story which described how Axel found the cave and what it looked like, and how he watched the stars, and would have liked to be able to live there too, as long as I could go back and see my parents and other people I liked whenever I wanted. It would have been too sad to be living there alone forever.

*A madman?*

During the daytime I mostly played outside, but when I learned to read well, I would read all night before going to bed. But when I was reading something I liked a lot, I would take the flashlight we had and cover myself up completely, and continue reading under the covers, shining the light on the page.

Yuriy Tarnawsky

I was told not to do it when it was found out, and mother said I was going to hurt myself by reading so much.

There was a madman wandering through the region at the time, and he would come strolling through the village from time to time, barefoot and dressed in rags, a big smile on his face and a long stick with lots of bells on it in his raised hand which he would shake so as to make them ring, followed by a group of village children, laughing and jumping, and making fun of him.

Mother said that I would grow insane like the man if I didn't stop reading so much, but terrified though I was at the prospect, I just couldn't break the habit.

Father scolded mother for saying such things to me, arguing that people didn't grow insane from reading, but agreed that I should read less because I might hurt my eyes reading in bad light, especially under the covers, keeping them too close to the page.

# 12

———

*An uprising?*

There was a peasant uprising one fall, and bands of men with heavy sticks, sharpened at the end, on their shoulders, carried like rifles, would go through the countryside, attacking rich people's homes and noblemen's manors, looting them and in some cases burning them down.

One night they appeared in our village and camped close to the manor in the field across the road from the schoolhouse that stood there at the intersection. They tore down the wooden fence with which the schoolyard was surrounded, and built a big bonfire with it, and cooked themselves food, and drank, and sang songs.

I could see the red glow from the bonfire rising above the tops of the trees from our home and heard the singing and laughter that accompanied it. Mother and Nora were white as sheet with fear and debated where to hide—under the bed or in the wardrobe—if we were attacked, but I was excited. I had my sword and father his pistol, and nothing bad would happen to us.

Father went to join the hrabia and some of the men who worked at the manor at the gate, which had been closed. (Adek and Bodek were not there because they were away in school.) They were armed with shotguns and some rode horses, so as to be able to better see over the wall in case we were attacked.

But the rebels showed no interest in attacking us, and in the end father and the hrabia went out and talked to them, curious to know what their plans were.

The men said they had no grievance against the hrabia and would leave in the morning. They were going someplace else.

Father and the hrabia then went home, as did most of the men, with only a couple staying at the gate, which remained closed.

*Your father went to sleep?*

On coming home, father changed into his night clothes and went to bed, although he left his pistol on the night table beside him. As I was falling asleep, I could tell from his breathing, though, that he was staying awake.

*The rebels left?*

The rebels marched off at dawn. They left behind the field littered with remnants of food, tin cans, and paper. A big black circle of ashes, embers, and unburned pieces of wood, wet and matted together, was left in place of the bonfire.  It had rained during the night.

# 13

---

*A game of polo?*

The field had been recently mowed and the hay cleared off, and Adek and Bodek were playing a game of polo on it against the hrabia and my father, the two, respectively, on Stan and Ollie, the hrabia on Marszałek, and father on Jan Amor, hitting a small round ball with wooden mallets on long flexible rods as they galloped along.

The boys wore hard round white hats with small black visors on their heads, red short-sleeved shirts, and tight white pants, the hrabia—a white cork helmet he usually wore when riding his motorcycle, a white short-sleeved shirt, and khaki riding breaches of the jodhpur type he wore while horseback riding, and father a regular white shirt with its sleeves rolled up and his jodhpur type khaki riding breeches he also wore while horseback riding. His head was bare. All four wore tall black boots.

The boys were much better at playing the game than the hrabia and father and were clearly winning, laughing and calling out in English to each other. They had learned playing polo during their time in England. Their school was starting in a few days and this was a chance for them to play one more game before going away.

*You were there with your mother?*

The day was warm and sunny, and mother and I had taken a walk together and had stopped to watch the game.

*Someone called?*

After watching the game for a while, I heard the voice of the hrabia's sister Anna calling his name, "Ka-a-a-a-a-rol! Ka-a-a-a-a-rol! Ka-a-a-a-a-rol!" coming from the direction of the manor. She had a peculiar way of calling people by hitting the palm of her hand over her open mouth as she called out their name. It appeared the sound carried farther when you did that.

After a while mother heard it too and remarked that the hrabia was being called, but she didn't want to interrupt the game.

The voice kept calling on and on however, and both mother and I began to feel uncomfortable about it, and mentioned this to each other, but then it stopped, and we ceased to worry. The reason for the calling had apparently not been that important.

Yuriy Tarnawsky

Shortly thereafter we heard the hrabia's sister voice calling out his name once again however, this time in a normal way, "Karol! Karol!" from close behind our backs.

As we turned around, we saw her running toward us, all flustered, her hair loose, an expression of desperation on her face.

We both got worried this time. Something serious must have happened at the manor house—a person got hurt or some other calamity of that sort had taken place.

Barely able to run, stumbling and out of breath, but still calling out her brother's name, she ran past us unto the field toward him.

Everyone had noticed her by then, the game stopped, and the hrabia galloped on his horse to meet her.

Intrigued, mother and I ran after her, and as we reached her, heard her say in a gasping voice that German troops had crossed the Polish border. The country was at war.

# 14

---

*Under the bushes again?*

The weather continued being nice, and a few days later, as I ran out to play in the morning, I saw the figure of a man stretched out on the ground under the rhododendron bushes below the terrace of the manor house where I had spotted Karolina for the first time. He was in a military uniform and I thought it was a German soldier who was hiding, planning to attack us.

With my heart in my throat, barely able to breathe, I ran as quickly as I could home, straight to my father's office to tell him about it.

We ran to our apartment, he got his pistol, and ran out to where I told him the soldier was, telling me and mother not to follow him but to stay inside and to hide under the bed if we heard the sound of shooting. Nora was in school, which had started a few days earlier.

We waited for a long time for the shooting to start, but as it wasn't coming, decided to go and see what was happening.

Yuriy Tarnawsky

We worried about father.

There was a group of people gathered around the spot where I saw the soldier, father, the hrabia, and Adek and Bodek among them. The two didn't go off to school because of the uncertain situation. Everyone was calm, though, and people talked in hushed voices to each other.

It turned out that it wasn't a German soldier but Polish, who was dead.

He lay on his back, his rifle at his side and a huge puddle of something yellow and shiny spread out on the ground next to him.

I thought it was his guts and the contents of his stomach that had spilled out after his belly had been ripped open, but it was actually a huge pile of cartridges. He had carried them, loose for some reason, in a canvas bag that lay next to him.

He was killed not by a bullet but by a knife stab in his side, and nobody knew who he was. After being stabbed, he must have tried to hide in the manor grounds, crawled under the rhododendron bushes, and died there.

There was suspicion that there were German commandos in the area, in spite of there not having been any shooting however, and no one felt safe any longer.

*Your father was not called up?*

Father packed his suitcase and sat day and night next to the radio, waiting for his mobilization order, ready to go at a moment's notice, but it never came.  The Germans were advancing so fast the country was collapsing.

# 15

_____

*The Germans?*

One morning rumor spread through the village that the Germans were coming and later that day, almost in the evening, a loud rumbling was heard from the road leading from the west and a cloud of dust could be seen rising above the trees from that direction. Everyone ran outside and stood by the manor gate at the side of the road, waiting for them to come.

There was father, and mother, and Nora, and me, and the hrabia, and his sister, and Adek and Bodek, and everyone else living at the manor, gathered at one corner of the intersection, and a much bigger crowd of people from the village in front of the schoolhouse at the other. Panna Adela wasn't among us. I think she was no longer living in the manor at the time.

For a long time the road stayed empty, but then something dark appeared from around the bend in it and proceeded toward us. Some of the people started shouting happily in Polish, "*Nasi jadą! Nasi jadą!*"— "It's our troops coming! It's our troops coming!"—but fell silent after a few seconds. It was clear they were not Polish soldiers but German.

*Different?*

Their uniforms were gray-green and not mustard-colored, and their helmets went down lower in the back and on the sides and were shaped differently on top. They all looked young and many had their sleeves rolled high up above the elbow, something I had never seen in a soldier before. It made them look fierce.

They came on motorcycles—alone and with sidecars—frequently with a gun looking like a big black pistol hanging on a strap from their necks across their chests, and a machine gun attached to the sidecar up front.

There were also cars shaped like boats, painted mottled tan, and brown, and green, with a big black spare wheel on the front hood, the windshield folded down, and more normal looking ones with their tops folded in the back, and armored vehicles, also mottled, their guns pointing skyward, and troop carriers the same color as the soldiers' uniforms, with their canvas tops in neat rolls behind the driver's cabin and the soldiers in them sitting primly on benches along both sides, clutching the tops of their rifles whose buts rested on the floor, facing each other.

They came to the intersection, and most of them turned left and proceeded toward the village, but some of them continued down the road past us, in the direction of a nearby town.

Yuriy Tarnawsky

*The hrabia left?*

Father stood on my left, and as I looked up at him at one point, I saw that his face was stern and lips pressed hard together, as when he was angry, and that his right hand was in the pocket of his jacket and that it bulged, as if he were clutching his pistol in it, which I knew was not true. It was merely balled in a fist. He had left the pistol at home.

Since we came out, the hrabia had stood next to him, but now he was not there. I couldn't see him anywhere else and wondered where he'd gone. Then, suddenly, after a while, sounds of a shotgun firing were heard coming from the direction of the manor and with them flocks of crows could be seen rising like wispy clouds of black smoke above the trees. He had gone to shoot crows, as he would do when angry about something. They were a pest and did a lot of damage to the crops in the fields, and this was his way of venting his anger.

The faces of everyone around me got worried, and people were looking around as if questioning each other silently what should be done.

The hrabia's sister then turned suddenly and, as if possessed, ran toward the manor gate. The shooting had to stop immediately. It could lead to something serious.

# PART TWO

---

## ARCTIC

# 1

_____

*You had moved?*

The Russians were driven out by the Germans and we moved to my parents' hometown and lived with my grandmother. The house my parents had been building, which was finished just before the war, had been taken over by the Russians when they occupied the country and when the Germans came they took it over and moved some military officials into it.

It was three stories tall, stood on a hill, partly hidden by trees, not far from grandmother's house, and could be seen from the window of the room we lived in. I would frequently watch it with my father's field glasses, staring through the window from the inside so as not to be seen by them. Big and mute while viewed through the powerful lenses, forbidding in their military uniforms, they moved in and out of the house like some superior supernatural beings permitted to live in a magical space we craved but were not allowed to enter. The house was one of the nicest in town and I had never seen it on the inside after it was finished.

Yuriy Tarnawsky

At times, the frail figure of a local girl, her hair in neat braids, dressed in the regional costume consisting of a richly embroidered shirt with puffy white sleeves, short, sleeveless tight-fitting tunic, and a full flowery skirt, sometimes with a multi-strand coral necklace on her chest, would be seen entering or leaving the place, who I instinctively felt was a traitor. She had abandoned us and was on the side of the Germans. Like everyone else, I would stare at her with disdain and not speak to her if I were to meet her in the street.

Father avoided looking at the house whenever possible and certainly never watched it through the field glasses.

*In one room?*

My parents' bed, the two night tables, wardrobe, psyche mirror, sofa, and my bed were all in one room and the three of us slept there.  It was big enough to accommodate all the furniture, and had in addition a ceiling-high wood-burning masonry stove covered with glazed green tiles standing in one of its corners, which I would press against, as if cuddling up to a loving person, after coming in from the cold in wintertime when there was a fire going in it. Nora's bed was placed in the room in which grandmother slept, and her piano stood in the living room. The two servant girls lived in a little closet-like room off the kitchen.

*Winter?*

We came there in wintertime and, it being in the mountains, it was very cold and the ground was covered with deep snow. The stream which ran in the back of grandmother's house was frozen solid and buried under the snow, looking like one of the roads on the outskirts of town which hadn't been plowed. The plowing, if it did happen, was done by a pair of horses pulling a big triangle made from thick wooden boards which moved the snow to the sides.

There were few people in the streets even in the daytime, and occasionally at dusk, when they emptied, a group of Ukrainian partisans—young men in short fur coats and hats, wearing tall boots and carrying the Russian submachine guns called *"finkas,"* with the big round magazine up front, slung across their chests—would be seen marching down the street, singing patriotic songs about freedom and raising Moscow and Warsaw to the ground. They would come down from the surrounding villages only when it got dark, as it would have been too dangerous to do it when the Germans were around. Local policemen in their black uniforms could sometimes be seen in their midst.

I imagined myself to be marching and singing with them.

*German patrols?*

German soldiers with rifles on their shoulders and bayonets hanging from their belts, wearing long overcoats and skimpy caps, often augmented with earmuffs, could be seen sometimes going from house to house investigating something, accompanied by a translator, usually a Jewish girl wrapped in a warm shawl. They appeared to be the most likely ones among the inhabitants of the town who spoke German.

*Christmas Eve?*

The first Christmas Eve, as we were about to sit down to the ritual dinner, a knock was heard on the door. It was surprising, for it was too early for caroling, but it turned out it was one of the patrols—a German soldier accompanied by a Jewish girl translator. A local policeman was this time also with them.

They asked if there were any Jews among us. Grandmother replied testily that there weren't, that we were all Christians and were about to celebrate Christmas Eve, pointing to the table which had been set. But if there were Jews among us, she added, they should be left alone. They were human, like Christians, and would have come to celebrate a Christian holiday together with us.

The soldier wanted to go through the house to investigate, but the policeman knew grandmother personally and said it wasn't necessary, and they left. We ate the meal in silence.

*What were the dishes?*

You always had twelve dishes, which stood for the twelve apostles. First came *kutya*, the ritual porridge of dehusked wheat kernels mixed with ground poppy seeds, honey, raisins, and nuts; it was followed by clear wine-red borsch served with *vuška*—little ears—dumplings filled with mushrooms; stuffed carp; three types of *pyrohy*—bigger dumplings, filled with mashed potatoes mixed with fried onion, sweet cabbage, and sauerkraut; *terčanyky*—large grated potato dumplings, also filled with mashed potatoes mixed with fried onion; *holubci*—little pigeons—stuffed cabbage with buckwheat; sauerkraut with peas; *suš*—compote of prunes, dried apple, and dried pears; *medivnyk*—honey bread; and finally *makivnyk*—poppy seed roll. No meat or milk products were allowed in the dishes, and all dumplings were served with a mushroom sauce. A layer of hay was placed on the table under the tablecloth and the dishes nested securely in it like birds in a nest. An empty chair and a place setting were set aside for those who couldn't take part in the meal and a bit of each dish was put on the plate in the course of the dinner, and a big sheaf of wheat called *didux*—great grandfather—stood on a stool in the corner.

*Caroling?*

Carols were sung by all in the middle of the meal as well as afterwards. Later, carolers, usually young boys and girls, carrying a big red, or yellow, or golden paper star on the end of a long stick with a lit candle inside it, called "*zvizda,*" meaning "star," would come and sing a carol or two. They were rewarded with money, apples, nuts, or sweets.

Yuriy Tarnawsky

*What happened at midnight?*

At midnight rivers flowed with wine and farm animals spoke in human voices to the farmer if he got to them in time.

*A tree?*

We had a Christmas tree and made the decorations ourselves—chains of strips of red, yellow, and golden paper glued together into interlocking rings, walnuts and apples and candy in their wrappers strung up on a loop of thread, whole eggshells with the egg white and yolk blown out, with angels and other figures painted on them, stars and angels made from blades of straw, and things like that.

These were augmented by glass baubles of different colors—gold, silver, red, blue—called *"ban'ky,"* bought in town, by little candles that were put into metal holders that were clipped onto branches, and by sparklers on long wires, called "Bengal fires," which were wrapped around branches to make them stand upright or hang down. The candles stayed lit for a long time, but the sparklers lasted only a short while, spewing out thick showers of sparks like fountains emitting jets of blinding-bright light. Hitting your skin, they didn't burn at all, which amazed me, and I was often tempted to let them land on my tongue, so that I could taste them, but never dared to try it, being afraid of getting blinded by a spark falling into my eye.

*Presents?*

We got our presents the night before St. Nicholas day, under the pillow. It was great to wake up in the middle of the night hearing the rustling of wrapping under the pillow or next to it. I wasn't allowed to open the presents until the morning however, but, excited though I was, would fall asleep quickly, knowing that they were there safe at my side.

Christmas Day, as we got back from church, we would look for coins and nuts hidden in the straw that was strewn over the kitchen floor.

# 2

———

*You went to school?*

I finished first grade before we moved to my parents' hometown and went straight to second grade when we moved.

The school was on the hill on the other side of town and I walked to it every morning, either taking the longer route through the center of town or the shorter one along its edge. I liked taking the latter not so much because it was shorter but because taking it, you had to walk under the viaduct and could see its arches repeating themselves like an echo in both directions, gradually getting smaller and smaller.

Going through the town was nice too because I would cut across the central square which was surrounded by buildings with arches on the ground floor you could hide under when it rained, and would catch the smell of bread and rolls being baked coming from the bakeries housed there. This route was always better in bad weather, especially in wintertime, when it had snowed during the night, since it would have been cleared of snow. It would be a while before they got around to clearing the other one.

*You loved school?*

I loved school, and would be sad if it was closed for holidays or for some other reason and even at the end of the school year before summer vacation. I remember crying one year as I was walking home from school after the closing ceremonies, sad at the prospect of not seeing my classmates all day and not doing things together, such as attending classes, doing gymnastics, singing, putting on plays, playing during recesses, and so on. But it didn't take me long to forget about school in the summer as there were all those other wonderful things I could do. In a couple of days my sadness was all gone. But when fall came, I was eager to go back to school.

*You were unruly?*

I was a pest at school, unable to sit quiet for a minute, answering questions asked of other students if they couldn't answer them themselves, and arguing with teaches about things I thought I knew better.

I was seldom reprimanded however, because mother taught at the school and father was in charge of things in town which included schools.

*You did your homework?*

Yuriy Tarnawsky

On coming home from school, I would do my homework right away, to have it out of the way, and then eat and go out to play. This way I didn't have to worry about having to do it later.

*Library?*

There was a library in town and I had access to books I had never dreamed of before. There were so many of them on the shelves that I was sure I wouldn't be able to read them all and thought how wonderful life was that I would never run out of something new to read.

There was also a bookstore in the central square and I loved going into it and looking at new arrivals as well as at the books I had seen before and liked. Some of those I would manage to convince my parent to buy for me.

*Books about Cossacks?*

The books I read then were primarily about the Zaporizhian Cossacks. We didn't have any books about Cossacks when we lived at hrabia Karol's estate, and I had heard just a little about them from my parents. Now there were many, and when I was taking out a book, I made sure it was about them.

Grandmother had two big pictures in frames behind glass hanging in the living room with Cossacks in them—one with many of them on horses, the hetman in the center with a mace in his hand and enemy standards strewn on the ground before him, gathered in front of a priest in rich regalia standing on the steps of a church with his hand raised high, blessing them, and another one with many of them sitting or standing while roaring with laughter, gathered around the figure of a scribe behind a table, writing a letter. They kept fueling my interest in the subject.

*Poles and Tatars?*

The books were all about Cossacks fighting Poles and Tatars, mostly the latter, which I especially loved because it dealt with people different from anything I had seen or heard of before. There was a story about a boy who was killed by a Tatar arrow as he was sitting high up in a tree reporting on them to the Cossacks below, and about a girl who led Tatars into a swamp where she drowned together with them rather than to her village which they wanted to pillage, and about a boy who went to Crimea looking for his sister who the Tatars had taken away to a harem, and about a *džura*—Cossack boy apprentice—who swam alone at night from a *čajka*—a Cossack longboat—to a Turkish galleon, got onto it, and blew up its gunpowder store, sinking the galleon and dying in the process himself, and many others like that.

I learned that the Cossacks were great scouts, crawling on their stomachs flat on the ground and reporting on the enemy and practiced doing it myself at home and outside, and that they communicated at night by making sounds like owls which I also tried, and that they could stay under water for a long time by breathing through a reed which I also tried but in which I never succeeded, and that they were fearless, and were not afraid of dying, and would smoke their pipes without a care while impaled on a pole.

I also learned that *"čykyrý baška!"* meant "off with your head!" in the Tatar language, and would yell it fiercely while knocking off with a stick the tops of flowers running through a field, as I had done with my sword when we lived at hrabia Karol's estate, pretending to be a Cossack chopping off the hated Tatars' heads. My sword had gotten lost somewhere by then during our moving, and it would have been too small for me anyway.

# 3

---

*Roundups?*

From time to time there were roundups of people in the town conducted by German soldiers with the participation of the local police.

People would be seen running in all directions, trying to escape or hide inside some courtyard or doorway, so as not to be captured.

At the beginning, I think, they were after Jews, to take them to the local ghetto or perhaps a concentration camp, but later after young men and women to send them to Germany to work as slave labor in factories and on farms.

*Ghetto?*

Part of the town was cordoned off and settled with Jews. They wore the six-point stars embroidered with yellow thread on their clothes and were controlled by Jewish police.

Yuriy Tarnawsky

*Executions?*

One cold, rainy afternoon in early spring, as I was going home
from school, I saw people rushing down the streets away from
town center.  Intrigued and worried, I asked someone what
was happening and was told that it was Jews being executed
by the Germans. People were running to see it.

Frightened as I was by the idea, I couldn't stop myself from
following the others and wound up on top of a hill outside of
town, in a crowd of people gathered on one side of a large pit
dug out in the ground. We'd had a lot of rain recently, it was
still raining, and I stood soaked through to the skin, up to my
ankles in mud.

Guarded by German soldiers and the local police, the Jews
stood on the opposite side of the pit in another crowd, trailing
off in a line. Those in the crowd were all dressed, but as they
joined the line, they would take off their clothes, throw them
onto a huge pile on the ground, and move slowly one after
the other toward the edge of the pit where a German soldier
stood with a pistol in his hand.  As someone would step up to
him, he would put the barrel of the pistol to the back of his or
her head, a loud cracking sound would be heard like a dry stick
breaking, the person would fall head-first into the pit, the next
person would step up, and the process was repeated.  This
happened very quickly and peacefully, without any of those
who waited or were shot resisting, as if having agreed to it
beforehand, and it didn't look as though the soldier was killing

people but was merely stamping their heads with a stamp like documents, certifying them for something.

I was shocked by what I was seeing, not so much by the notion of killing as by the mundane way in which it was done, and also by the sight of the naked bodies, all deathly pale and deformed, as if seen through tears, with the black unruly clumps of body hair on them, especially those of women, which I had never seen before, but as if hypnotized was unable to tear my eyes away from what I was witnessing. There must have been children among the victims, but I don't remember seeing them, as if they'd been hidden by the size and appearance of the adults.

Then, unexpectedly, I felt a sharp pain in one of my ears and realized that someone had grabbed me by it and was pulling me away.

It was a tall man with a stern expression on his face.

"What are you doing here, boy?" He said in an angry voice, pulling me away from the crowd and pointing me in the direction of town. "You shouldn't be seeing this. Go home!"

Shamed, like a dog with its tail between its legs, without any resistance, I obeyed him and followed the road into town.

*You told your parents?*

Knowing I had done something wrong, I didn't tell anyone I'd been to see the execution, but that night I ran high temperature and, unable to hide my feeling of guilt, in a fit of shaking and crying, confessed what I'd done, convinced I was being punished for my deed.

I was told it was wrong for me to have gone to witness the execution but was assured that my getting ill was not a punishment for it except a result of my getting wet and chilled. It did turn out that I had pneumonia once again however, and, as before, I had the dreaded nightmares about my tongue being a plain, strewn with big sharp boulders which I tasted and kept running into, but it wasn't as bad as the first time, and I didn't have leeches put on my skin, and was cupped only once, and stayed in bed for only two weeks, and after that went back to school more or less fine.

Mother had been bringing me my homework, which I did diligently, and I wasn't behind the rest of the class when I went back.

*Another execution?*

It was the next year, or perhaps the one after that that I witnessed another execution—this time, it was said, of Ukrainian partisans.

Like the last time, it was a cold, cloudy day, although it didn't rain, and as I was walking home from school, I was caught up among people being herded by German soldiers and local police toward the central square. During regular roundups they would leave children alone, but this time I was forced to go with everyone else.

I was afraid we'd all be sent to Germany to work as slaves, but it turned out that we were only to witness a hanging.

Gallows was set up in the middle of the square—two tall, thick wooden posts joined by a heavy beam on top, with a raised platform between them.

As we stood, watching, a truck with German soldiers in helmets and with rifles, with some men in civilian clothes among them, drove up and stopped by the gallows.

The Germans got out first and helped the men, whose hands were tied behind their backs, get down from the truck, led them to the gallows, and made them climb a little ladder onto the platform and stand in line under the beam. There were five of them and they all did this obediently, again as if carrying out a task they'd agreed to previously, and waited patiently for what was to come. They were bareheaded and wore regular civilian clothes, with the necks of their shirt collars open under their chins.

There were five thick ropes with nooses on the end hanging down evenly spaced from the beam and each man stood under one of the ropes. One of the Germans went from man

Yuriy Tarnawsky

to man, putting the noose over his head and tightening it around his neck, leaving the knot and the rope in the back.

Having done this with all, the German stepped aside, a loud noise sounding like a hammer hitting something hard was heard, the board the men were standing on collapsed under them, and they all fell down a foot or so, and then shot up a little, jerking up and down and twisting from side to side. The heads of all of them were tilted to the side in a strange way, as if they'd all also agreed to do this previously.

As was the case with the execution of Jews, I was shocked not so much by the notion of being killed as by the everyday nature of it. It had happened so peacefully and quietly, without the men protesting, which didn't seem right.

After about a minute or two, the hanged men became quiet and hung limply on the ropes rotating from side to side, as if trying to get a better look at the crowd.

This disgusted me for some reason, and unable to bear the sight, I turned around, pushed my way out of the crowd, and hid behind one of the pillars of the arches surrounding the square, pressing my back against it.

I didn't stand there long when, suddenly, I saw my father before me with an expression of amazement on his face. He asked me in an angry voice what I was doing there, and when I explained to him what had happened, he didn't say anything but took my hand and proceeded to lead me out of the square. The crowd had started to disperse by then and nobody stopped us from leaving.

Later I learned that the men hanged were not partisans but civilians picked at random who were executed in reprisal for a German soldier having been killed by partisans.

4

———

*Buried alive?*

Stories were floated constantly about people being buried alive. Coffins would be dug up and signs of violent struggling would be discovered inside, pointing to the body having been buried alive—scratches on the lid and sides of the coffin, clothes shredded, cheeks furrowed with finger nails, with flesh under the latter, eyes torn out, lips chewed up, fingers bitten to the bone. To prevent this, a mirror was to be placed at the alleged dead person's mouth and if it steamed up, it meant the person was alive.

*You had related dreams?*

I had many recurring ones. If the mirror was covered with soot, it was a proof the person was dead. Huge black galleons with black sails sitting on top of hills would be boarded by dead people dressed in black, carrying black umbrellas and suitcases, who would wave with big smiles on their faces as the galleons sunk into the ground the way ships sink into water while being launched. Dead persons in coffins would come speeding down steep slopes covered with wet slippery grass laughing and cheering like kids sledding in snow in wintertime.

Skeletons with arms on each other's shoulders forming a circle would dance the spirited mountaineer *arkan*—lasso—dance.

*Holy week?*

I liked all religious rituals, such as those at Christmas time mentioned earlier, those at Easter, consisting of going to the Resurrection Mass while it was still dark, seeing the sun rise as *"Xrystos voskres!"*—"Christ has risen!" was sung to the exuberant tolling of bells, kissing everyone who was near you three times on the cheeks while calling it out yourself, and especially celebrating the following "Wet Monday," when people threw water on each other, as well as those of "Green Holidays"—Pentecost—when the insides of homes were decorated with branches full of shiny young green leaves. But more than anything I loved those of the Holy Week.

It was great to try to fast with the adults Monday through Saturday, not to drink the whole day and eat only stale bread, boiled potatoes, and sauerkraut flavored with caraway seeds and sprinkled with sunflower oil, stand in the church at night for hours listening to the tragic story of Christ's Passion accompanied by mournful singing, and not hearing the sound of church bells starting with Thursday, but instead the hammering of wooden mallets on boards hung up on chains under the eaves of the church. Boys were encouraged to do that, and I stood with others, pummeling the resonant board with a mallet in each hand as hard as I could, my arms raised high, until I couldn't hold them up any longer.

There were also wooden clappers consisting of a handle, a piece of board in the form of a circle on one end, and a little mallet that struck it as you shook your hand. Kids carried them around all day, rattling away with glee and determination, filling the air with the loud sound of clapping.

The jarring sound of wood hitting wood repeated rapidly and without end carried all over the town and the surrounding landscape, reminding everyone for those three days of the true nature of life hidden under joy and everyday bustle during the rest of the year.

*Majivky?*

Each evening throughout the month of May, while the sun was still up, there were services devoted to Virgin Mary called *"majivky"*—May services—conducted in the church, which I loved to attend. For almost an hour you stood in a crowd of people, mostly kids of the same age as you, many your classmates, singing together endless chants praising her virtues, in which a phrase was repeated over and over with a new word each time inserted in the same spot into it, until you stopped thinking and did it automatically, having ceased to be yourself and turned into an inseparable part of the group. You stood there opening and closing your mouth and emitting a stream of sound out of it, your nostrils filled with the sweet smell of incense and your eyes with the sight of its bluish wisps wafting lazily in the dim light streaming in through the windows. When the service stopped, and you went outside, it was like waking up from a dream.

Out in the open, it'd already started to get dark, and there were *xrušči*— maybugs—buzzing around in the dusky air and among the thick young green leaves in the trees, and the bodies of those crawling on the ground, in their hard shells, crunched like dry twigs under your feet as you walked down the sidewalk.

Girls in pairs, threesomes, or even higher numbers walked around, desperately holding hands, as if afraid of being snatched away by some evil force.

*Flagellations?*

There was a little chapel with thick whitewashed masonry walls, the figure of Christ on the cross on one of them, in which no more than four or five people could fit, which we discovered one day on a hill outside of town while playing after school. It seemed abandoned, with a bunch of withered flowers and stubs of burnt-out candles on the altar and all sort of debris on the floor. Possessed at the time with religious fervor, I convinced my friends to clean it up, and we would come there whenever we could, light candles, burn some dry weeds as incense, sing religious songs, and flagellate ourselves. Each of us made a whip consisting of a stick with a bunch of pieces of heavy rope with knots tied into them on the end of it, and we would take off our jackets and shirts and hit ourselves on the back as hard as we could while singing.

A wonderful feeling of purity would come over me afterwards, such as I imagine an empty room with windows open and flooded with sunlight would feel if it were capable of feeling, and I was willing to go on with the practice forever, but one by one my friends lost interest in it and wouldn't come, and so in the end I stopped going there too. Flagellating yourself alone wasn't at all the same as doing it with others.

*Sleepwalking?*

Another common story was of people walking in their sleep in the moonlight.

If you were to go out on a clear moonlit night and walk through the town, you could see all around human figures, mostly women, balancing themselves carefully, their arms extended before them, as they walked stiffly along the ridges of rooftops. Their eyes and faces would be blank, and they weren't aware of what they were doing, and if you were to call out to them or in some other way wake them up, they would fall and hurt themselves or get killed. It was thought that the reason they were doing this was because they wanted to get to the moon, walking along its light as if along a road.

There was a woman in town, the wife of a prominent doctor, who, it was said, was a sleepwalker and because of that was shunned by some, as if she were ill with a dreadful disease or had committed a grave crime. She had walked around with a bandage around her head at one time, and it was rumored she'd hurt herself after being woken up while sleepwalking. I would meet her occasionally in the street, pale-looking and sullen, and was afraid to come too close to her, so as not to be infected by her affliction.

One night, however, I found myself awakened, trying to open the window in the room we slept in, drenched with white light streaming in through it, being shaken by my father. The moonlight had reached my bed and made me get up and try to climb outside without my being aware of it. My getting up did wake up my parents however, and father, seeing what I was doing, jumped out of bed and got to me in time.

I don't know what I would have done had I managed to get outside, but I remember seeing the field beyond grandmother's garden white in the moonlight, which rose above it like a vast pyramid of light, and I was probably planning to climb along it to its top.

Frightened though I was at what had happened, deep inside I was proud about myself. I had always wanted to be different from other people, and this was a proof that I was.

# 5

----

*Pan Atrament?*

Pan Atrament—the name meant "ink"—was a photographer, an acquaintance of my grandmother, whom I got to know well. He had many books and would let me look at them or take home to read.

He lived alone in a home of his own, not far from grandmother's, with his big black female dog called Camera Obscura, or simply Obscura. She was old and gentle, and slept most of the time stretched out on the floor, almost merging with it like a puddle of water someone had spilled. In summertime she liked doing it outside, under the gooseberry bushes that ran in a long hedge facing the side of the house. I loved gooseberries and would have my fill of them when I was visiting pan Atrament, but he didn't bother picking them and when they ripened, they fell to the ground, forming big murky yellow puddles. Obscura liked them for some reason and would select the biggest puddle there was, make herself comfortable in it, and go to sleep. If you called her, she would graciously open her big sad eyes with a wide expanse of white around the irises, look at you for a second or two, and close them again, sinking back into her delicious senile slumber.

Pan Atrament would sometimes take me with him into the darkroom lit by red light and show me the way pictures are developed. I was amazed at how he conjured complex images to appear out of noting on a blank sheet of paper he turned around in water with his hands, like a magician in circus pulling objects out of thin air. It was nice to watch him, but I never wanted to do it myself. The worlds I liked were those created with words.

*Stereoscope?*

Pan Atrament had traveled widely in Europe and in addition to books had a big collection of photographs of his travels that were meant to be viewed through a stereoscope.

They were arranged neatly in small wooden boxes, a pair of identical ones on each stiff card, and when you put them in the stereoscope and looked at them, you saw a tiny real world which it seemed you could step into and live.

There were pictures of Paris, with its tall iron tower, churches, bridges, squares with tall columns or statues in the middle, and a wide boulevard framed with two rows of trees, a big arch at its end, those of Rome, with its churches and ancient ruins, of London, with a long building along a river, a square tower on one end that had a huge clock on top of it, of a small beautiful palace in Germany, and of the city of Leipzig and the art collection in its museum, as well as others.

Yuriy Tarnawsky

I particularly liked the pictures of the art collection of the Leipzig Museum and would frequently ask to look at them, and one day, mixed in among the pictures, I found photographs of naked women standing, sitting, and lying in different poses. Except for what I'd witnessed during the execution of Jews, which was now for me just a confusing blur, vision marred by huge black and white snowflakes, I had never seen naked women before and was shocked by the images— their unblemished white skin, the perfectly shaped hemispheres of breasts, the gentle curves of hips, and especially the black triangles of hair at the bottom of the abdomens where the legs met—but, although feeling I shouldn't be doing it, went on looking. The sensation they evoked in me was unlike anything I'd ever felt before and I couldn't stop myself from continuing.

As I was doing it, at one point I realized pan Atrament was standing behind my back, watching me. He must have been there for a while without my realizing it. Cringing, I began to turn my head in his direction, planning to excuse myself somehow, but then felt him put his hand on my shoulder and laugh softly in his deep voice, saying, I shouldn't worry and could go on looking. There was no sin in seeing a woman's naked body. Just like the objects in the collection in the museum, it was a beautiful work of art.

I was a boy, he went on, and would also enjoy seeing the images for reasons other than artistic beauty. When I grew up, he concluded, I would understand why.

# 6

---

*Rivers?*

There were two rivers running through the town—a small one, Vechir—meaning "evening,"— which was more of a stream than a river and which ran in the back of grandmother's house, as I had mentioned earlier, and a bigger one, Natalka— "Natalie,"—which cut through the center of town. Vechir flowed into Natalka, and Natalka into the big river we used to go to before the war while visiting grandmother, I also talked about earlier. We never went to it together any more however, probably because of the war. It was not the time for picnics.

If the weather was fine, which it usually was, every day of the two months of school vacation, July and August, I spent with other boys on the Natalka, swimming, catching fish, and playing. I would go there straight after breakfast, go home for lunch, return, and stay until supper. Sometimes we wore our swimming trunks while there, but most of the time ran around naked. In the fall, when it was time to go back to school, I was the color of copper head to toe, and my hair was bleached flax-white.

Yuriy Tarnawsky

I had many friends, mostly my classmates, but my best friend was a boy named Askold, who was in my class and was the same age as me. I spent most of the time with him.

Askold's father was the chief engineer at the local power plant and they lived in the apartment at the facility. The plant was on the bank of the Natalka, on the edge of town, and we usually stayed there. The Natalka was mostly wide and shallow, but at that spot it was narrow and deep, and was good for swimming and catching fish. The spot was also handy in that it was close to Askold's home and we could get there quickly if something was needed.

*Who taught you to swim?*

I don't remember how I learned swimming, but it must have been by myself, on the Natalka, watching other boys. At first, I just paddled along dog-style, like everyone else, but later learned to swim breast stroke, which we called *žabky*—frog-style—I saw mother do when I was little, as well as Cossack-style, with one arm under the water, going back and forth, and the other one above it, swinging forward over the head and plunging down, to pull along with the first one.

*How did you fish?*

We fished with our hands, or with long sticks sharpened at the end like spears, or simply stones. Catching fish with a fishing rod was too boring. It was for adults who had the patience to stand still for hours and wait for the fish to bite. We had too much energy for that.

You caught fish with your hands where the bank was steep and the water had carved out little niches in which fish liked to stay. You had to explore the bank with your hand very carefully, so as not to scare the fish, and when you found a niche, go into it slowly, and if there was a fish in it, caress it gently with your fingers for a while so that it'd think they were water, and when it got used to it, put your hand in the proper position, in the middle of the body, and close it quickly and hold tight, so that the fish wouldn't get away. They were slippery and often would slip out of your fingers when you thought you had them caught. When you caressed them, they felt like weeds swaying gently in the water.

The niches the fish stayed in were often deep under the water, and sometimes just your mouth would be sticking up above it as you looked for one with your hand. At other times you had to go in under water completely and find a niche and catch the fish before you ran out of breath.

You speared a fish with a stick, sharpened on one end, where the water was shallow and it was forced to swim close to the surface, with its back almost sticking out. You had to aim the stick at the middle of the body, and drive it in hard, and make sure it went in deep, which was difficult.

Yuriy Tarnawsky

But the hardest was to catch a fish by hitting it with a stone. It was like with the stick but it was more difficult to aim with a stone and you had to throw it real hard, so that it'd stun the fish. Some boys were able to do it, but I never did.

I did catch a fish once, though, by throwing myself over it and pinning it down under me. It was big, with a large head and a long feathery tail, and was sunning itself where the water was very shallow so that the top of its back was sticking out above it. It was perfectly still and seemed to be dozing. I saw it from afar, and quietly snuck up on it and threw myself down on it with my whole body, grabbing it with my hands. It was struggling desperately, trying to get away, and I had a hard time holding onto it, but luckily, I had my shirt on and was able to hold it against it, so that it couldn't get away. Had my chest been bare, I'm sure I would have lost it.

I threw it down on the pebbles far away from the water, where it kept thrashing about desperately, jumping up and down, curving this way and that, its silver body flashing in the sunlight. It looked like it was going to do it forever, so I grabbed it and held it down with my hand against the ground while it struggled, and hit it on the head with a rock until it grew still.

I saw other boys do it sometimes with fishes they caught, so I thought I'd do it too. I felt proud at having done it. I would have considered myself a sissy, had I not been able to do it.

*You ate what you caught?*

Most of the fish we caught we would clean and grill over a fire we built on the pebbles among the osier bushes, holding them over the flames on spits made from thin sticks. They tasted delicious, the meat flaky and sweet without any salt on it. You just had to be careful with the bones.

Askold's father had two short knives made for him and me at the power plant workshop and leather scabbards by a shoemaker in town, and we wore them proudly on our belts, and used them for cleaning fish—opening them up and getting rid of the innards, and then cleaning off the scales.

The big fish I'd caught, though, I took home, by carrying it over my shoulder, strung onto an osier shoot, that went into its gill and out through its mouth. We had it for supper that night.

*You played with boats?*

Boats were the big thing with all of us, especially me and Askold.

I was at first in third and then in fourth grade at the time and, having exhausted the books on Cossacks, was reading everything I could lay my hands on. But I especially liked books on travel to distant foreign lands and looked first of all for those. To get to those places you had to cross seas and oceans, which sounded exciting, and I began dreaming about

Yuriy Tarnawsky

being a sailor myself. I would even walk like a sailor sometimes, with my legs wide apart, swaying from side to side as if on a rocking boat. The reason Askold's father had the knives made for us was because I came across the word *kortyk* in one of my readings and asked mother what it meant, and she explained it was a short straight sailor's knife. I loved the way the word sounded, and when I said it to myself, it was as if I held the knife in my hand and therefore would often repeat it over and over. I told Askold about it, and that's how we got those knifes.

We would build little sailboats out of boards, drill holes, and put sticks into them for masts, and attach pieces of paper or cloth to the latter for sails, and would sail them on the quiet parts of the river. Askold had also once a boat made for us out of sheet metal by someone at the plant, but it was too heavy and wouldn't float.

But the best were little boats you could buy sometimes which had a tiny boiler with a tin foil membrane on top you poured water into. You lit a short piece of candle, and put it in a spot under the boiler, and when the water boiled, the membrane would vibrate, and steam would come puffing out of two little pipes under the boat, propelling it along. The trouble was the membrane would break quickly and there was no way to fix it. And after a while you couldn't buy those boats any more.

*Other games?*

There were huge iron tanks sitting in the power plant yard, which were meant to be buried in the ground to store oil in them. They had big round openings on top that made them look like submarines. We would climb into these and pretend we were submarine sailors. But after a while we were prohibited to do this. There was a danger of one of us getting hurt.

The last year we played there, I recall, apparently at the suggestion of one of us who had learned more about sex than the rest, we made a little mound out of clay at the edge of the river, smoothed it out with water, made a hole in it, and one by one tried to stick our little members inside. You were supposed to derive pleasure out of doing it. None of us did however, and we never tried it again.

*And Vechir?*

Vechir was too shallow to swim in and was for times when I was going to school. I did play on it sometimes with my friends, especially Askold, but mostly I did it alone. It was close to home and I could stop what I was doing and in a few minutes be there. Much as I loved playing with others, I also enjoyed being alone.

Big old willow trees grew along one of its banks, leaning over the water, and I would climb up on the favorite one I had, which leaned far out, watch the water flow below me into the unknown, and dream.

As I had imagined the waters of the brook that ran through the park at hrabia Karol's estate we lived in when I was little arriving at the shore on the other side of the ocean, I imagined those I looked at then eventually reaching the shores of the Mediterranean—Greece, Italy, Spain,—North and South Africa, the Americas, India, China, Japan. I smelt the salty air of the seas they traversed, felt on my face the hot sun of the tropics that had warmed them, heard the harsh sounds of the languages spoken in their proximity, and saw the colorful clothes and exotic features of the faces of the natives in the ports they'd arrived at reflected in them.

The favorite time was fall, when the willow trees shed their leaves. These were long and narrow, curved up high on both ends and bright yellow, looking like gilded Venetian gondolas as they were carried along by the current. I imagined being on a canal in Venice in one of them, propelled by a gondolier moving a big oar in the back, taken someplace exciting, or being a gondolier myself, standing on the platform at the back and moving the oar, perhaps taking a beautiful girl to her destination. I could also be standing at the window of a palazzo, peeking furtively out from behind a heavy curtain of moss-green velvet at a gondola sailing by with a beautiful lady in it I was secretly in love with, perhaps being in return loved by her.

This was as good as reading books, and I never got tired of it.

# 7

---

*Pani Afrodyta?*

*Pani*—missis—Afrodyta was my schoolteacher. She was the wife of another doctor in town and knew both of my parents. I would see her sometimes in the corridor between classes talking to mother or to father when he came over as part of his job. She was extremely beautiful, I felt the most beautiful woman I'd ever seen, and I was deeply in love with her. When she smiled at me or praised me for something, which happened often, a feeling akin to a swoon would come over me and it would take me a while to come back to normal. I couldn't take my eyes off her when in class and thought about her constantly when out of it.

They lived in a house with a big garden surrounded by an iron fence on the bank of the Natalka next to a bridge close to the center of town, and possessed with a need to see her, after school or on Sundays or holidays, I would sometimes go and stand on the bridge, leaning onto the railing, my eyes on the garden, hoping she would come out and play with the dog they had or with her teenage daughter so that I could watch her. This did happen occasionally, and I would let then the images of her moving and doing things seep into my consciousness, and when she went back inside, go back home pacified.

One day, I think in middle of the week, after school, as I stood on the bridge, my head turned in the direction of her home, praying with fervor she would come out, I felt a pair of soft hands cover my eyes from behind and a melodious voice ask, "Guess who?"

I didn't I recognize her voice nor even acknowledge it was a woman's, but instinctively felt it was her, and terrified at the prospect, stood frozen, unable to speak.

Laughing and helping me to turn around, she said it was her, my school teacher, and added that she was surprised I didn't recognize her.

And then, as I continued standing speechless, she took my head in her hands and, tilting it back, bent down and looked straight into my eyes. From close up, hers looked like two giant diamonds sparkling among the long eyelashes.

She said my eyes looked just like my father's and were beautiful, and then bent down some more and kissed them.

I don't recall what happened next but we never talked about the incident afterwards, as if it'd been erased out of our minds, and the relationship between us continued exactly as before, which I felt was right.

# 8

_____

*Aunt Eda and uncle Genko?*

Aunt Eda—Edyta—and uncle Genko—Evhen—were mother's cousins, so they weren't really my aunt and uncle but that's what we called them. Aunt Eda lived in the center of town off the main square, in an apartment on the third floor with big, high-ceilinged rooms with tile-covered masonry stoves in the corners, taller and nicer that those at grandmother's, and a balcony off one of them. To get to the place, you had to climb creaky stairs in a dark smelly staircase. I hated the latter but enjoyed visiting the place because of the balcony, which I loved to stand on and watch the street below, and the sweets I was often given as well as, in winter, big sweet- and sour-tasting apples with a rough golden skin called *renety* that were lined up along the edges on top of the stoves to make them ripen better.

Aunt Eda lived alone with a couple of servant girls, but her brother Genko, who was single, having never been married, for some reason frequently stayed at her place despite having an apartment of his own in the police headquarters where he worked. He had a high-rank position but for some reason seldom wore his uniform and usually went around in civilian clothes instead.

Aunt Eda had been married and she and her husband were arrested by the Russians shortly before the latter were driven away by the Germans and were held in a prison with many other people in a nearby town. One by one people were taken away for questioning and would not come back. Nobody knew what happened to them but it was assumed they were either executed or shipped to prison camps in Russia. Aunt Eda's husband was one of them.

One day, while waiting to be questioned, aunt Eda found part of a human finger with a nail on the end in the soup or stew she was served. The meals they were given were usually meager but from time to time there was meat in them and everyone was looking forward to those. It looked as though the dishes were prepared with the flesh of the people that were killed.

A few days after that the Russians fled and Germans occupied the town and aunt Eda was spared from being killed. The body of her husband was later found in a mass grave. It hadn't been touched but parts of those of some of the others were missing. The Russians had indeed been serving human flesh to the prisoners.

Aunt Eda, similarly to the doctor's wife who walked in her sleep, was sullen and pale, and I ascribed it to her having eaten human flesh. Despite liking to go to her place, I was deathly afraid of being touched by her.  She was infected with the disease of having eaten human flesh and I didn't want to catch it.

During the Polish occupation uncle Genko was involved in antigovernment activities, was imprisoned, and tortured in a variety of ways.  One of them, it was said, was being forced to drink manure liquid.  He was also beaten with a plank with a nail on the end which penetrated his skull and injured his brain. There was a huge muscle-like lump on the nape of his neck and he walked with his head bent forward and turned to one side like a bull in the process of charging. He was also prone to sudden outbursts of unexplainable violence and behind his back was called *"narvanyj"* — "unhinged." All of this was  attributed to the tortures he'd been subjected to.

# 9

———

*Empty homes?*

Walking through the town you would see here and there homes which were empty. They had belonged to Jews and no one had moved into them yet.

We had been offered one ourselves as a compensation for ours, but father refused to take it. I would walk pass it when taking the shorter route to school and was glad we didn't live there. It was old and shabby and belonged to someone else. I couldn't imagine it being our home. It was nice living at grandmother's, and we had a beautiful place of our own which we would move into one day.

It was forbidden to go into these homes but some of the boys in class had been breaking into them and would brag about it, and so one day Askold and I decided to try it too. There was such a home not far from grandmother's, on the bank of the Vechir, and we decided to break into it.

It faced the street that ran along on the other side and so as not to be noticed, we went into it from the stream side, wading through the water. The house had a glassed-in veranda in the back and the door to it was open. The door from the veranda into the house proper was open too and we got inside without having to break anything.

The place was empty of furniture and stuffy from being closed up for a long time. There were dust balls on the floor everywhere and things scattered all over it, such as items of clothing, sheets of paper, kitchen utensils, and so on, among them one of those little black leather boxes with something written in Hebrew on parchment inside with straps attached to it Jews use for praying. In one room we found a wooden box with small square glass plates neatly stacked up in it. When we took them out, we saw they were photographs of oriental-looking people—Chinese or Japanese—some individuals and couples, but mostly families, standing in big tightly-packed groups facing the camera, looking like giant swarms of bees that had decided on a resting place. We couldn't find an explanation for why they were there.

The place smelled bad, like the bed of a sick person, and there was something scary about it, and we decided to leave right away. I would have liked to take the box of photographs with me but decided against it. Having it at home would have meant I had made the place part of my life.

We walked out the way we came in but rather than wading through the stream walked past the side of the house into the street. There was an empty lot a few houses down and in it two men were carving up the carcass of a huge steer or a cow lying on the ground. They walked around it carefully as if around a big bonfire, afraid of being burned.

*Kalmyks?*

The Germans were being stretched thin on the two fronts and had begun to recruit into service men of nationalities ruled over by the Russians. For a while there was a detachment of Kalmyks quartered in our town designed to keep order. I remember seeing them marching down the central street and singing in Russian about wide fields and "our" cavalry riding horses over them, in which "our" had obviously replaced the original "red." Strangely, many of them had blond hair and red slanted eyes.

On Christmas Eve of that year two young local men from one of the neighboring villages accompanied by a girl, who had been forced laborers in Germany, had arrived by train for the holidays and were walking home, trying to make it to the ritual dinner. They were stopped by a Kalmyk soldier and as the men tried to defend the girl from being raped by him, he killed them by stabbing them with a bayonet. The girl was ultimately let go and reported what had happened to the police.

The incident took place late at night, in the dark, on a road outside of town, and the girl was unable to identify her attacker. The killed men were not from the same village as she and she didn't know who they were. They had met as they were walking out of town. Their bodies were taken to the morgue in the cemetery and stayed there a few days until the men's identities were established.

The news about what had happened spread through the town, and people were going to the morgue to look at the bodies.

Askold and I heard about it too and decided to visit the morgue ourselves. It had snowed during the night and the path to the morgue from the cemetery gate had not been cleared. We trudged along it laboriously, our feet sinking deep into the snow or getting caught in the footmarks made by the people who had walked before us. My heart was pounding louder and louder with my every step as I was nearing the building, but I was unable to stop myself from proceeding. The lure of seeing what lay ahead was too strong to be overcome by my fear.

The morgue was not guarded by anyone and we stepped inside, closing the door behind us.

Except for the two bodies, the place was empty. The men lay stretched out on their backs on two tables next to each other, bareheaded but fully dressed in heavy overcoats, their eyes shut and their arms at their sides. They looked very much alike, like brothers, with thick, straight sand-colored hair combed back and full faces. Their lips were closed and their cheeks bulged as if their mouths were full of water and they were trying to hold it in, but it seemed that it was silence that they were holding in actually. It looked as though a lot of it had gathered in their mouths. They both must have been stabbed in the abdomen or the sides, but you couldn't see where. The overcoats were masking it. One of the men, though, had in addition a big stab wound at the side of his neck under the jaw. The blood in it had hardened and turned black, looking like sealing wax that was meant to plug up the hole.

Surprisingly, the fear I had been feeling was now gone. The sight seemed normal like the snowy landscape I had seen before coming inside and there was nothing frightening about it. I looked at the bodies calmly, observing and recording the details, as if writing them down on paper. After a while, I realized I had seen all there was to see and that there was no point in my staying on. I had been expecting to witness something extraordinary, but it was clear that nothing of the sort was coming. I was time for me to leave. I turned toward Askold and saw an expression on his face similar to mine. We stood there a few more seconds and then turned around and walked out of the morgue.

A couple of men were trudging their way down the path toward the morgue we had taken earlier and we made room for them to pass.

*A photograph?*

There was a photograph of the four of us—father, mother, Nora, and me— taken by pan Atrament, I think in late March of that year, sitting on a sofa at the foot or the big bed with the Ukrainian trident—*tryzub*—on a shield high up on the wall above the headboard behind us. It's different shades of gray in the picture but was gold on pale blue in reality.

Father is sitting on the right side of the sofa, his right elbow resting on its arm, his legs crossed, the tall boot on the right one, which is on top, reflecting a strip of white light coming in through the opposite window. Nora is sitting next to him, wedged into the space between him and mother, turned slightly toward her. Mother is sitting straight up with her knees pressed together and her left arm around me, as I sit partly in her lap and partly on the arm of the sofa, clutching a big book while pressing it to my chest. You don't see the title of the book in the picture but it was a condensed children's version of the *Iliad* and the *Odyssey* I was reading at the time, which I found fascinating. We all have calm expressions on our faces, but mine is close to smiling.

It was the last picture of the four of us together.

# 10

_____

*Your father went away?*

Later that year father went away to join a military unit that was to fight on the side of the Germans against the Russians.

There had been talk about it for a while and then the day finally came. He was going to take the train in the middle of the night to go to where the recruits were gathering and he lay down beside me on the side of the bed as I was going to sleep and talked about what he was doing.

The Russians had killed millions of our compatriots just before the war and we had to make sure this wouldn't happen again. As an officer, too, it was important for him to upgrade his military expertise so that he could better lead others in any future fight against our enemies. Being trained by the Germans would do that.

I was to not misbehave, listen to mother, stay healthy and strong, study hard, and write him about what I was doing. He would be thinking about the three of us all the time, would write to me in turn, and when the war was over would come back and then everything would be as before.

He lay still after speaking and I fell asleep to the sound of his breathing, feeling the warmth of his body flowing into mine.

When I woke up in the morning, he was no longer there but it didn't seem bad at all. It was going to be as it'd been when he'd go away for military training during the summers when I was little—he went away to be a soldier and to defend our country, as was his duty, and would come back to tell me about it. I had my books, my school, my friends, my mother, sister, and grandmother, and would wait for him to return.

*Where did he go?*

He went first to a training camp where they trained everyone— officers and regular soldiers—and then to an officer training school, to be brought up to the German army standards.

The first camp was in some forest with tall, thin pine trees, as it looked in the photographs, and he said the training there was very hard. They had to get up at five o'clock every morning, and he'd come back at night with his shirt sopping wet with sweat, so that he'd have to wring it out.

At the end of this training, he came home on a brief furlough hollow-cheeked, but strong-looking, a peak cap on his head, dressed in a German foot soldier's uniform and heavy nail-studded military boots, his pants tucked into woolen socks, and a bolt-action rifle slung over his shoulder. He slept for twenty-four hours without stopping and then slowly thawed out to normal behavior. He brought us some candy and dried fruit mashed together and shaped into small chewy bricks and other things like that he'd purchased at the commissary, and when he left, it was more difficult than when he went away the first time. He'd been gone for a long time, was with us just a few days, and now would be gone once again for God knows how long.

*Officer training school?*

Right after that he went to an officer training school at another camp, farther away West. It was also in a pine forest but the pines there were different—thicker and gnarled in places, with the branches on top bunched together into a canopy. Those in the first camp were straight and looked more like fir trees. The soil there was sandy. He sent us a picture of him lying on his side and looking into the camera in a patch of white sand among short, sparse grass, with pine trees up a slight slope above him, their tops looking like flat black umbrellas. The training there was hard too but he had been toughened up and didn't find it as difficult as before.

He came for a longer furlough this time, tall in a tall officer's hat with a shiny black visor and a silver skull on a black strip going around it, a long overcoat with wide lapels, tall black boots, and a pistol in a holster on his belt. The skull looked like an evil silver rose. The pistol was bigger than the one he had before the war, with a long nozzle and a scored brown handle, and it was hard for me to hold it in one hand while pointing at something. Hanging in the holster on his belt, it looked swollen like a badly sprained hand in a leather glove. There were three silver stars on the black patch on the collar of his tunic on the left side, and a silver lion standing up on its hind paws, its front ones thrust out menacingly before him, on the right one.

He brought even better things this time—chocolates, tangerines, and a couple of bottles of French wine among others.

*More furloughs?*

I think he came back on a furlough one more time before being send off to the front but I don't remember much about it. It must have been similar to the previous visit and the novelty had worn off.

*Photographs?*

In addition to the photographs from the two training camps, there were others, such as he standing in the center of a group of soldiers from his company, a field hat with flaps on the sides and a long cloth visor on his head, wearing a short tunic, riding breeches, and tall boots, a pair of binoculars hanging down from a strap on his chest and a pistol in its holster on his belt, some of the soldiers with submachine guns looking like long pistols, hanging on straps slung across their chests; he sitting in the front passenger seat of one of those cars that looked like boats I saw Germans coming in at the outset of the war, the windshield of this one not folded down however, the driver, who was his orderly, behind the steering wheel, both of them with their heads turned left toward the camera; and he sitting on a horse, wearing a cap and earmuffs, a long warm overcoat, and heavy boots, in a snowy landscape with a black strip of a forest behind him.  This last one was from an expedition his unit went on to hunt down Russian partisans in the northwestern part of the country.

*Letters?*

He wrote to all three of us—to Nora and me individually and to mother for the benefit of us all, often, and almost on a regular basis, responding promptly to the letters we sent.  His were quite long, at times covering two or more pages, traced out in neat lines in his surprisingly small and cramped, but perfectly legible hand, describing what he'd been doing and dealing with the topics we'd brought up.  Mother often complained that I was being unruly, so he would admonish me but it was clear from his wording that he didn't think I was doing something unacceptable for a boy of my age.  I should simply tone down my behavior and try not to annoy mother.

I loved the fact that he had an orderly, and that the latter was devoted to him, and that the soldiers in his company would come to him for personal advice, and that he was receiving commendations from his superiors. The horse he was shown on in the above photograph was bay and he simply called it *"Hnidyj"*—bay—because he was going to have it only for a few months. I was disappointed he didn't drive the car himself but that was the norm—officers had more important things to worry about than to make cars go in the proper direction.

When the weather got warm, they were sent off to the eastern front to directly face the Russians. His letters got much less frequent then and since mother's health had deteriorated badly, what he would have written to her he addressed to grandmother.

# 11

------------

*A film?*

One day mother took Nora and me to see a film about German colonies in Africa being shown at the town culture hall. I hadn't seen any films before, and the subject of Africa sounded fascinating, and so I asked mother to take me to see it. She agreed and decided to take Nora too. At that time father was already away in the army.

The film was German, with narration in that language, there were no subtitles, and I didn't understand much of what was happening on the screen, but just couldn't tear my eyes away from it. In the middle of the showing I felt an urge to urinate but not wanting to miss a second of the film, I stayed on in my seat and wound up wetting my pants. That didn't faze me however, and I watched the film to the end, absorbing every frame of it like dry sand sopping up drops of water being poured on it. The impenetrable jungle, dark as the night, its giant trees, monkeys in them swinging on lianas, huts with thatched roofs, built out of thin sticks, the nearly naked people with black shiny skin, short clinging hair, soft facial features like bread soaked in water, women with naked conical breasts, men carrying long bows, narrow sharp-pointed shields, and spears, some adults small like children next to the tall blond white men.... It was unbelievable what the world was like! Even my most exuberant stories were no match for it.

I went home drunk with what I'd seen, dreamt about it all through the night, and next day, from the moment I got up, pestered mother to take me to see the film again. The screening had been on a Saturday and there was another one on Sunday.

As she had done years ago with the circus and the dwarf elephant, after some hesitation, she relented and took me to see the film again. Nora declined the offer to go along. She had her piano and her girlfriends.

I enjoyed the film as much as the day before, if not more, but in the middle of it mother got sick and decided to leave. I was torn between staying and leaving, but in the end the choice was made for me. Mother passed out in the lobby, an ambulance came to take her to the hospital, and I was taken home.

*An operation?*

Mother came home from the hospital the next day but she didn't feel good and didn't go back to work, feeing worse every day, and after a couple of weeks went back to the hospital and underwent an operation.

Yuriy Tarnawsky

The operation was difficult, and mother stayed at the hospital for almost a month, and when she came back, she went straight to bed.

My bed was taken out of the room where I had slept and put in the living room and another bed, narrow and tall like those in a hospital, was brought in and put in place of mine, and mother stayed in it from then on.

She hardly ever got up and when she did, would walk holding onto things and dragging her feet, and after doing what she'd set out to do would go back to bed right away.  When she got up, she never put on her regular clothes but would pull a bathrobe over herself and stick her feet into slippers to make it easier for herself.

She ate very little and was losing weight and looking paler and paler every day.  It was summer by then, and the weather was getting progressively warmer, and her growing thinner and paler seemed to be part of the summer setting in.

# 12

---

*Her looks?*

She was getting paler at first but with time she started to turn yellow, like what happens to paper as it gets old. She began to look like an Egyptian mummy, one of those, pictures of which I had seen in books. Her arms and legs were thin sticks ending in big tumor-like bulbs where they joined other. Her neck was a bundle of sinews pushed into the big container of her skull which seemed a pot turned upside down and empty inside. Her hair became straight and stuck out at the end like frayed straw. It was dull and matted from not having been washed. Her nose became curved like the beak of a predatory bird. The cheekbones seemed to have pushed their way up toward the eyes, as if trying to move in their place. The eyes bulged as if indeed being pushed out to the surface by the cheekbones. They were huge.

They seemed like the ends of bones which fit into sockets protruding out of the sockets of her eyes. They seemed to have gained weight while the rest of her body had lost it. Actually, her teeth also seemed to have gained weight, or it was possible that there had gotten to be more of them. At times, when she opened her mouth, it seemed it was full of teeth, as if someone had shoved a fistful of them inside it and left them there. Sometimes they seemed to be all jumbled up. It seemed sometimes she was smiling when she opened her mouth to say something because of her teeth having gotten so numerous and big. Also, because of all these changes, it seemed at times she had gotten younger. She looked then like the fifth member of our family, her own daughter, younger than either Nora or me.

*The room?*

The room smelled bad, similar to the Jewish house Askold and I had gone into, but even worse, like the mouth of a person who hasn't brushed his or her teeth in the morning or who has bad breath. It was her body and the chamber pot that hadn't always been quite emptied that was the cause of the smell. You had to open a window in the room to stay inside it.

*Eating?*

As I said, she didn't eat much, so attempts were made to find food which she'd like. These were things that were very hard to get, such as oranges, grapes, watermelon, and even wine. I remember a bottle of French pink sparkling wine which I suspect father had somehow managed to send us. But she'd just touch them and set aside, saying she'd eat them later, which she never did. She took just a few sips of the French wine and some of it flowed out of the corner of her mouth, hanging there like a strip of pale raw meat so thin it was translucent, barely chewed on.

When I was with her, sometimes she'd try to force me to eat what she'd left, which I found revolting. I remember a slice of watermelon, dark green on the outside with a thin ring of white next to it, followed by a big segment of pink that got progressively redder toward the center where it was the color of red-hot embers. She had taken a few bites out of it and left the rest on a plate on the table next to the bed and asked me to finish it. Reluctant, I picked it up gingerly and bit into it, but it felt slimy, as if coated with her saliva, and I retched trying to swallow it.

She saw it, looked at me with those eyes of her bulging like ends of bones out of her eye sockets, and with her mouth full of white teeth screamed that I was a bad son because I was disgusted with her.

I swallowed what I had in my mouth and somehow managed not to throw up.

*Screaming?*

When she wasn't sleeping, she'd usually just lie still stretched out under the sheet looking straight ahead with unfocused eyes, not having energy to move, but sometimes, in fits of despair, would sit up and scream in a screeching voice about how all of us treated her badly, thinking she would soon die, but that she wasn't going to die, and would get better, and would then pay us back for having been bad to her. She'd get well, and leave us all, and go travelling to wonderful distant countries she hadn't been able to see, and wouldn't bother coming back.

*You read to her?*

Sometimes at her asking, and sometimes on my own, I would read to her, sitting in a chair next to the bed, having left the window open to make sure the room didn't smell bad.

Occasionally, she'd say a word or two, commenting on what I'd read, but usually would just lie still, stretched out under the sheet, her head sunken into the pillow, staring ahead and listening. Frequently, after a while, she'd fall asleep, and I would stop then reading and go away. But at times, I'd go on reading on such occasions, even though I knew she was no longer awake. For some reason it felt good.

I tried to read to her from some of my favorite books which I owned, such as *Robinson Crusoe, The Children of Captain Grant, Gulliver's Travels, Jungle Books, Tom Sawyer, Huckleberry Finn,* and the condensed, children's version of *The Iliad* and *The Odyssey,* but she didn't care much for them. *Robinson Crusoe* and *The Children of Captain Grant* were about people stranded on a desert island. *Gulliver's Travels* was weird and there were descriptions in it of decrepit old people who wouldn't die, which reminded her of herself. *Jungle Books* was about a boy who lost his parents and was raised by wild animals, which she hoped wouldn't happen to me. *Tom Sawyer* and *Huckleberry Finn* dealt with unruly boys like the one I was sometimes. *The Iliad* was all about war, which is what we were having, and *The Odyssey* about a husband who took a long time coming home from the war, which she hoped wouldn't be the case with father. She did like a little the passage from *Jungle Books* dealing with the abandoned maharaja palace, and I would read for her sometimes from it. The talk about the luscious jungle in it seemed to invigorate her. But what she really liked was Sven Hedin's *Travels Through Asia*, which I was constantly rereading by myself, the two volumes of which I took out of the library and held onto as if they were my own, and so in the end I read only from them. It had attracted my attention because the author was Swedish, which connected it in my mind with *Axel's Cave*.

She liked the description of the travels in general, but we settled in the end on what she enjoyed the most—the part dealing with the Tarim river, where it's described how the expedition traveled in boats down its winding course through the changing countryside ranging from impenetrable poplar forests, through thickets of reeds many feet high, to bone dry deserts, visiting towns and encampments, meeting interesting people, and ending in the mysterious lake of Lop-Nor.

*Sewing?*

A few times mother gave me sewing lessons so that I could sew things for myself when she was gone. These were sewing on a button, darning a sock, and mending a tear.

I brought whatever was needed, sat down on the chair next to the bed where I always read, and did things as she told me.

For buttons, you threaded the needle through the four holes as close as possible to an equal number of times, wrapped the thread around the threads between the button and the cloth so that they were like a rope, pushed the needle to the other side of the cloth and then a few more times through the place where the thread was bunched up so that it stayed in place.

In darning, you went back and forth across the hole in the sock in one direction, forming close parallel lines across the hole, and then went across them, going under and over the parallel lines with the needle, as if weaving a mat.

Sewing up a tear, you did it on the inside part of the garment, stitching close together and leaving as small a seam as possible, and then flattened it by pounding it with something hard.

We repeated each of the tasks a few times and in the end I could do them well.

# 13

_____

*The Natalka?*

The weather was unbelievably beautiful around that time, with cloudless skies and scorching hot sun day after day, and I would spend every minute I could with my friends on the Natalka.

There was an abandoned grist mill a little way down the river from where we bathed, with the channel that had funneled the water that turned the wheel dammed up at the entrance. The other end had been left open however, so that there was a narrow pool of stagnant water along the bank with the spot around the wheel much wider and quite deep.

The water there was greenish-yellow like engine oil and full of algae, and huge eels had bred there, swimming around peacefully in it, undisturbed by the presence of anyone on the bank.

We would sometimes go there trying to fish but they were extremely hard to catch. I think it was perhaps only two or three times that one of us had managed to do it during all the time we'd tried. They were too slippery to hold on to and too quick and sinewy to spear. I never managed to catch one myself.

*A strange boy?*

As I said, there was a group of us, all friends, that would gather on the Natalka, but one day a strange boy, tall and with a white skinny body, who I assumed was a friend of one of the other boys, appeared among us, judging by what he intimated, coming from a nearby village. At one point we decided to go fishing for eels and he came along.

Some of us jumped in the water and went exploring with their hands along the bank but were unable to catch anything. The boy then said you had to dive in deep because that's where eels like to stay. He said he knew that because he'd done it many times and would show us now.

As we looked on, he jumped in the water head first with his arms outstretched, and went in deep, so that you couldn't see even a trace of his body. We waited patiently for him to come up but time went on, and there was no sign of him. We thought at first this was because he was an expert fisher and could stay under the water for a long time, but time went on and he still wasn't coming up. Then someone said he'd noticed bubbles coming out of the water a while back and that that must have been air escaping out of the boy's lungs, and that he had drowned.

We began debating whether this was true, but eventually everyone realized too much time had passed for the boy to be still alive, and everyone grew panicky, and didn't know what to do. Some suggested some of us should jump in the water and try to pull his body out, but others said it was too dangerous and that we should get help from an adult. There was no question by then he had drowned.

Askold and I then ran to the power station and told his father what had happened, and he came back with a couple of workers, and they pulled the boy's body out of the water.

He was held up feet first and was shaken violently, a big gush of water came rushing out of his mouth, he was laid down on the ground, mouth to mouth resuscitation was tired on him and his chest was pumped, but he didn't regain consciousness.

They left him lying on his back stretched out on the ground, long and pale, his white body smeared in places with black dirt, his face indifferent, as if bored, faint cold glitter coming out through a crack between his eyelashes.

It turned out nobody knew who he was. He didn't come with anybody but apparently just joined in as he saw us frolicking in the water. I don't know what happened to him next and who he turned out to be.

*The Vechir?*

Yuriy Tarnawsky

Grandmother's neighbor's cat had a litter and they wanted to get rid of some of the kittens. They had given away two, and there were five left, which nobody wanted. They were asking around who would be willing to drown them, but nobody wanted to do it either.

I heard about it and volunteered. This was my chance! You had to be tough to be a man, and this was a way to prove to myself and others that I was.

They were given to me in a box and I carried them to a little footbridge on the Vechir not far from grandmother's house. It was in the middle of the day, but there was no one around. We lived close to the edge of town.

I went to the middle of the bridge and rested the box on the handrail. The kittens were crawling around in the hay at the bottom of the box—black, spotted black and white, and gray. Their eyes were still closed and they were weak on their paws, reeling as they crawled, unable to keep up their heads steady, like old people, and emitting pitiful pleading cries.

As I looked at them, all of a sudden, I was seized with an incredible hatred—for them being so small and defenseless and for making such pitiful sounds, and so I seized one of them by the tail, swung it around in the air a few times, and hurled it into the water.

The current was slow and the surface of the water smooth, and the kitten broke it and stayed visible for a second or two, but then sank under the water and didn't come up. The ring it created on the surface spread, getting less and less noticeable, and in a few seconds was gone.

I did the same with the next two, one of which popped up its head above the water for a few seconds before going down, and the other two I just grabbed by their bodies and threw as far as I could, giving each of them a real hard squeeze, as if wanting to cause them pain and perhaps even damage. Their bodies were hot, especially underneath, along their bellies, and the warmth stayed on my fingers like soft feces. The feeling was disgusting and I had an urge to wash my hand.

I wasn't told what to do with the box and originally thought of taking it back home, but now wanted to be rid of it as soon as possible, and so I threw it in the river and ran off the bridge, hoping to find something to occupy myself with, so as to forget what I'd done.

# 14

_____

*Germans retreating?*

The Russians were making big advances on the eastern front
and the German army was retreating.

Day after day, columns of soldiers in tanks, troop carriers,
trucks, autos, wagons, motorcycles, on bicycles, horses, and on
foot flowed like an endless current of slow-moving lava down
the narrow traffic-choked two-lane highway that ran past the
town, heading west.

Askold and I would stand for hours watching them like a live,
three-dimensional film run for our benefit, among a crowd of
children and adults. Dust churned up by the caterpillar tracks
and wheels rose up from the gavel-packed road, hovered
above it, and settled on the surrounding area. The leaves on
the trees in orchards close to the road and the fruit in them
looked white, as if coated with flour. We would cough from
time to time from the dust getting inside our throats and spit
out gritty, brown saliva, and as I would look at Askold through
my own dust-coated eyelashes, saw his were white, as if he
were an albino. For some reason the dust on a person's hair,

skin, and clothes wasn't as noticeable. After leaving, we would take off our clothes, and shake them out well, and wash up ourselves in the river.

An attempt had been made to camouflage some of the vehicles with tree branches, but these were usually meager, and couldn't possibly have served the intended purpose. Besides, these vehicles were in the middle of a river of others, most of which had no camouflage on them, so the attempt to make them inconspicuous looked silly even to a boy of my age.

I was fascinated by the different kinds of vehicles, uniforms, and arms that you saw. First, there were tanks, some huge, other smaller, then something that looked like a cross between a tank and a truck—a long vehicle with a pair of wheels up front and caterpillar tracks behind them, with an open area behind the driver's cabin in which soldiers sat. Some of these had a big canon up front, others sometimes pulled a cannon on its own wheels behind them. Then there were trucks that carried troops and sometimes pulled a cannon behind them, topless passenger cars, some looking like boats, others closer to a regular car, motorcycles with or without sidecars, and horse-drawn wagons, undoubtedly confiscated from local population, but driven by German soldiers. Horses on which men rode wore saddles, so they were probably military horses, and most of the bicycles were olive-green, so were also probably of military make.

The vast majority of soldiers wore the standard German gray-green uniforms, although many were also dressed in mottled camouflage outfits. It was hot, so some had taken off their jackets and wore just shirts unbuttoned on the chest and with the sleeves rolled up. But there were also troops in dust-blue uniforms and some in pure black. I liked these the most, for they seemed the fiercest. They were all tank personnel, and I remember them standing straight up, sticking out of the turret of a tank, blond and young-looking, like evil young angels, in their black uniforms with the silver markings. I wished I could be one of them.

As to arms, in addition to canons, there were the regular single shot bolt type rifles, submachine guns that looked like big pistols, big submachine guns with and without two legs up front, bazookas the Germans called *Panzerfaust*—tank fist,—things that looked like flame throwers, and so on.

*Trains?*

The Germans were also retreating in trains.

These were extremely long, and it might take one of them a quarter of an hour to go by, and consisted of freight cars, at the open doors of which stood soldiers calmly looking out, intermixed with flatbed railcars, carrying canons and all sorts of vehicles, including tanks. Standing next to or sitting inside some of these, once again, you could see soldiers calmly surveying the landscape. The expressions on their faces seemed to tell they were glad to be going home.

*Hospital train?*

One day I saw a train at the station that was different from the usual ones—it consisted exclusively of passenger cars, and through the windows of these you could see inside white horizontal strips, looking like beds stacked up one on top of the other. It was stopped and German soldiers, some with bandages on their heads, shoulders, chests, or arms, were leaning here and there out of the windows, buying fruit and berries from the local women who had brought them from the nearby villages.  It was one of the hospital trains that was carrying wounded soldiers to Germany.

Some of the women were going into the cars to do their selling, and I decided to take a look myself, to see what it was like there.

It was a world different from the one outside.  The interior of the car was all open, and there were three-tier bunkbeds set up diagonally along its length, with narrow aisles between them.  Men, some partly dressed in uniforms, others in their underwear lay on the beds, at times covered with sheets, some stretched out on their back, others on their sides, still others propped up on their elbows or sitting up.  Some were also standing or moving in the aisles or in the passageway along one side of the car.  There was white everywhere—white sheets, underwear, and bandages, with an occasional red stain here and there, where blood had soaked through the gauze.

It was stifling hot, and the smell of medicine mixed with something sickening hung in the air. No one was talking, and the silence rang in my ears like a soft endless whining sound made by someone in great pain. It was interrupted occasionally by a stifled moan coming from different areas of the car.

Spellbound, as if charmed by something beautiful, I walked down the passageway, looking around, unable to tear my eyes away from what I saw, when, suddenly, I felt the car heave with a jerk. The train was moving!

A soldier standing next to me, dressed in uniform, turned to me and said something urgent in German. I caught just a few words—*Bubi,*—boy—*steig aus,*—get off—and *Deutschland*—Germany. He was obviously urging me to get off the train, or else I would wind up in Germany.

By then the train was already moving, and like possessed, I ran back to the door through which I'd come in, jumped into the air, and rolled, as I hit the ground.

Chills ran up my spine and my hair stood on end as I came to a halt and prepared myself to get up, and I swore never to do anything so stupid again.

# 15

_____

*Vechir again?*

War was invading minds and lives of everyone, and my friends and I were no longer spending much time on the Natalka. Instead, I went back to my faithful friend, the Vechir, and would play on it for hours by myself or sit in the willow tree, musing, while watching the water under me flow by.

As I was doing it, one afternoon, I heard a voice coming from the direction of grandmother's house calling my name. It was a high-pitched female voice, and it went on and on, flying through the air like an incredibly long whip, first unwinding, then curving gracefully this way and that as it stretched, until reaching its full length, and finally cracking with a sudden jarring sound of silence.

I had been expecting something like it for a while now and knew with certainty what it meant, and deliberately refused to react to it, as if pretending it wasn't there, and only when it stopped, slowly, as if tired, climbed down from the tree and wended my way home. I didn't walk along the road but through fields and backyards, winding up in the back of grandmother's house.

Looking over the fence, I saw that the window to the room in which mother lay was open, and so I got into the yard, went up to the window, and climbed through it into the room.

Mother, as always, lay on her back, stretched out full length under the sheet, but this time it was pulled over her head so that not even her hair spreading on the pillow above her was visible.

With my heart in my throat, I think, walking on tiptoes, I went up to the bed, pulled the sheet down and up a little, and looked under it.

Her face looked better now than it'd looked the last few months—fuller and softer, with the facial features smoothed out by an expression of peace. She no longer felt pain. Her nose was still thin and curved sharply as before however, and her eyes bulged huge under the closed eyelids. I looked at her for a few seconds, and then concluding I'd seen all there was to see, pulled the sheet back over her face as it'd been, and this time definitely on tiptoes, went up to the window, and climbed into the yard.

I clambered over the fence and, once again wending my way through fields and backyards, got into the fields outside of town, climbed up a big hill that was there, lay down in the tall grass growing in it, and watched clouds way up in the sky above me flow somewhere as the water had done in the Vechir a short while ago.

I stayed like this for a long time, and only when it got late, went back home, walking in through the front door.

Grandmother and Stefa were there waiting for me, but they said nothing, clearly aware I already knew what had happened.

Nora was probably in her room, crying.

# PART THREE

---

# NIGHTS

# 1

---

*Who was Stefa?*

Stefa was a distant cousin of mother who came to help out with taking care of her after she came back from the hospital, replacing the two servant maids who were let go. She moved into the small room off the kitchen where they had been staying.

She had been living with her mother in an apartment in town and had a little boy named Yurchyk who was about a year old. She got recently divorced from her husband who moved to another town.

It was impossible for the boy to live with us and he was left in the care of his grandmother. Stefa would frequently drop in on them during the day when it was possible however, although she slept at our place.

*And your father?*

Yuriy Tarnawsky

Father was on eastern front. As mother's situation worsened, a telegram was sent, informing him of that and asking for him to come. Normally he would have been permitted to do it, but the Russians had started a big offensive right then and when mother died, the unit he was in was encircled and we didn't know of his fate. All we knew was that they were trying to break out.

*The wake?*

Next day mother's body was washed, dressed, and laid out on a table in the living room for viewing. Two women I didn't know came to help grandmother and Stefa do it. I remember sitting in the living room watching them going in and out of the room where she lay, taking things in and out, always making sure to close the door behind them.

Mother lay in a coffin dressed in a long black dress with a big white collar like a giant daisy around her neck, a rhinestone brooch pinned to her chest. She had a similar real diamond one and although there was talk of pinning it on her to go in the grave, it was decided to substitute it by the rhinestone one someone had. We would need the money. On her feet she wore black stockings and black shoes. Her hands were crossed on her chest, the right one over the left, so that the wedding band on her finger showed, and her head rested on a white pillow, with some white lilies arranged around it. It was a miracle that any were found on such a short notice. Her hair had been washed and combed and once again looked wavy

162

as it used to, and she looked peaceful, although less so than she'd appeared to me when I saw her under the sheet.

Toward the evening, people started to come in to show their respect, some of them staying on.

Food and alcohol were brought out, people ate and drank, talking at first about mother, but gradually more and more about other things. A deck of cards appeared, people—men—started playing, there was laughter and loud banter, and this went on for the better part of the night.

I slept in our room, alone in the big bed where father and mother used to sleep.

*Funeral?*

The funeral was held the next day in the afternoon.

The priest with his attendant came, a brief service was held over the body, and as the coffin was being nailed shut, everyone sang the mournful *"Vičnaja pam'jat'"*—Eternal Memory, repeating it three times.

People around me were crying but hard as I tied, I just couldn't. It was as if I'd lost the way to the source of my tears. I could tell they were there, but simply couldn't find them. Upset, thinking that people would say that I didn't love mother, I asked Stefa who stood next to me to give me a real hard pinch, so that I would cry, and when she heard it, she gave out a loud sob, put her arm around my shoulders, pressed me against herself, and we stood this way until the singing stopped, she crying and I continuing to stay still.

A hearse apparently couldn't be found, so the coffin was put on a wagon which was pulled by a single horse. The church attendant, carrying a cross, went first, followed by the wagon with the coffin, then the priest, grandmother, Stefa, aunt Eda, uncle Genko, Nora, and I.

A fair number of people came to the ceremony at the house, pan Atrament among them, but more joined in as we went through the town. Notice of the funeral had been printed at the local newspaper press and copies of it were nailed onto telephone poles—small white rectangles with a thick black line around it, a cross on top inside, with some text underneath. I watched for them as we went down the streets, and felt glad each time I saw one.

The cemetery was on the opposite side of town and to get to it, we had to travel a short distance along the highway along which the Germans were retreating. Luckily, they were going the other way, so we were able to proceed, and when someone blocked us, they would quickly get out of our way. There seemed to be curiosity mixed with sadness on the faces of those Germans who watched us go by.

You had to climb a hill to get to the cemetery, and finally we were there. The grave had been dug next to the grave of my grandfather—mother's father—who died the day I was born, and a surprisingly small mound of mustard-colored earth stood at the side of it. I had expected there would be more. For some reason it reminded me of a bush in the fall whose leaves had turned yellow, under which you can find shelter from wind.

A much longer service was held over the coffin this time, with *"Vičnaja pam'jat'"* sung three times once again, the coffin was lowered into the grave, holy water was sprinkled on it by the priest, we all threw flowers inside, and the grave diggers who had stood on the side all this time, waiting, began throwing the earth onto the coffin. It made a dark, hollow sound as it hit the lid.

I had looked inside the grave when I threw my flower and, seeing the coffin, once again was surprised by how small it looked. It seemed it should be bigger.

A small, neatly shaped mound of earth was built up over the grave after it'd been filled and a simple temporary cross of white wood was driven into the ground at its head. The wreath that'd been brought along was placed on top of the grave together with the remaining flowers, and everyone went away.

# 2

---

*Your father?*

Almost as soon as we got home, the door opened and father stepped in, accompanied by half a dozen soldiers from his company. They had managed to break through and had made their way to town by walking and hitching rides for a couple of days. The remnants of their unit were to meet in a village close to the neighboring Hungarian border, and they were heading there. It so happened that the road everybody was taking went through the town.

For a second or two I didn't realize who he was—some strange German officer at the head of a group of soldiers, all heavily armed with pistols, and grenades, and submachine guns—but then one by one began to discover under the layer of dust and sweat with which his face as covered the features I had known since childhood, which meant so much to me—the steely temples, the thin straight nose, the vertical cheeks, the chiseled mouth, the deep cleft at the tip of the chin, and finally the luminous gray eyes, slowly brightening with an oncoming smile.

I called out, "Father!" almost exactly at the same time as Nora, we both ran up to him and threw our arms around him. He lifted both of us up at the same time, pressed us to himself, and held us there.

My chest was pressing against the submachine gun that hung off his neck, and it dug itself painfully into my ribs, but I didn't mind it, and was willing to stay this way forever.

Suddenly, I found myself crying, and it seemed like everything was right again.

*The cemetery?*

Father wasn't surprised by the situation, having expected it from what was said in the telegram, and decided to visit mother's grave right away. He regretted they had taken a day off from their travel to rest up, for otherwise he would have been there for the funeral. All of us, as well as his companions, wanted to accompany him, but he insisted on going alone. He just drank a tall glass of water before departing.

The men washed up in the garden at the pump, having stripped naked from the waist up, soaping themselves well with a big chunk of homemade brown soap grandmother brought out and drying off with towels she provided, and father did the same on returning.

*Sleeping?*

Yuriy Tarnawsky

The bed mother had lain in was taken away, father slept in the big bed alone, with the door to the room closed, I in my bed in the living room, and the men with me, on the floor.

In the morning, the men departed, two of them going into the hills, to join the partisans, and four to meet the remnants of their unit, to where they'd been going.

Father decided to stay on for a couple of days to take care of the situation at home.

# 3

_____

*Night visitor?*

That night, as we were getting ready to go to bed, there was a knock on the front door and a man I had never seen before stepped in.  He was let in by father who, it appeared, was expecting him but who, judging by the words they'd exchanged, was also seeing him for the first time.

The man was tall, the same height as father, and was dressed in civilian clothes, in a jacket, jodhpurs, and boots, but wore a pistol on his belt on the left side, which stuck out from under his jacket. It wasn't of the German kind you most commonly saw, but like that carried by Hungarian officers, in a big holster with a wide flap over it, which hid the outline of the gun.

After shaking hands, the two retired to the room where father was staying and shut the door. It looked like they'd be there for a while.

Grandmother, Nora, and Stefa went to bed in their rooms, and I, already wearing a night shirt when the man came in, turned off the light and went to bed myself.

Yuriy Tarnawsky

I lay on my back, stretched out under the covers with my eyes open, staring into the vague outline of the living room illuminated by the soft light filtering into it through the frosted glass panes in the door, hearing the muffled sounds of the conversation, unable to fall asleep.

Before going to bed, I was able to make out that they were sitting on the sofa, facing each other while talking. Something about the man's visit worried me, but I couldn't figure out exactly what. I was sure however, the result of his coming would be something I wouldn't like.

Eager to find out what they were talking about, unable to withstand the temptation, I climbed out of bed, squatted down by the door, pressed my ear to the crack between its two wings, and tried to listen in.

I couldn't make out every word being said but gathered that the talk was about Russians, Russian partisans in particular, about a military unit being formed, the need for someone to lead it, and one of the neighboring villages. It seemed that members of Ukrainian intelligentsia were being arrested and some killed by the Russians in the newly occupied areas, and it was vital to prevent this.

The tone of the conversation suddenly changed, they got up, and it looked like the man would be going away.

I quickly ran to bed and climbed in under the covers.

In a few minutes they both came out, father led the man to the front door, they said good-bye, and he came back, going to his room.

As he was walking by, I asked him what was happening.

He came over to me, put his hand on my head, stroked it, and said not to worry. Everything would be alright. He then bent down and, as he would do sometimes when I was little, pressed his forehead to mine with his left eye directly over my right one and fluttered his eyelids, so that they tickled mine. It was a game we called "butterflies," and I was supposed to flutter my eyelids too, which I did.

# 4

___

*Stefa?*

He turned out the light in his room, and I thought he was going to sleep, but after a while, as I started to fall asleep myself, he came out and, walking on tiptoes, went into the kitchen.

I thought again that he was going there to get a drink of water, but I heard the door to Stefa's room open, him go in, and close the door.

Somewhat perturbed, not understanding what this meant, I lay with my heart pounding loudly and finding it difficult to catch my breath.

Time went on, and nothing was happening however, and I gradually relaxed and fell asleep.

*You had a dream?*

I had the following dream.

I'm in the middle of a vast, flat, snow-covered plain, stretching all the way to the horizon, were it curves down before disappearing. It's as if I'm high above the ground and can see the earth's curvature.

It's at night, and although there's no moon, I can see perfectly clearly as in the daytime. The sky above me is deep black and is covered with stars, which are clustered together in places like sand that hasn't been evenly spread. That must be the reason why I can see so well—it's the light from so many stars that makes it bright.

I must be finding myself in the southern hemisphere because in one spot in the sky the stars form a cross—the Southern Cross. On second look, it doesn't look like a cross of stars because it's all fiery—it's a cross of fire, although I still think of it as the Southern Cross. Suddenly, it looks scary to me, being all fire, and I turn around, so as not to see it. I observe that it's the cross that must be part of the reason why it's so bright—good part of the reason, more so than the stars.

I'm dressed in a shirt and pants and am barefoot but in spite of it being at night and with snow all around, I don't feel cold. There's just invigorating freshness in the air like on a cool summer night. My feet also don't feel cold in spite of my standing in the snow. It feels fluffy and soft around and under them, and actually makes them feel warm. I start walking, and feel it fly out from under my feet like fine feathers—down.

Yuriy Tarnawsky

Relaxed, I throw my head back and look at the sky.  The Southern Cross is behind my back now and all I see are myriads of bright stars in the vast expanse of the black sky. It's like what I used to see while trying to fall asleep on the bench on the terrace at hrabia Karol's estate when I was little, although I don't make this connection in the dream.  The sight is absolutely breathtaking and I can't tear my eyes away from it. The sensation is overwhelming, and I feel it'll never go away. How could it, when the sky is so incredibly beautiful?

But then I feel pain in my toes.  It's as if something were nibbling at them.  I stop, look down, and see that in fact there are little round black and white creatures gathered around my feet—about half a dozen of them at each foot, biting my toes.

They look like little baby seals, with black eyes and black spots around the mouth and nose, but white over the rest of their bodies, except with no flippers, round, and the size of snowballs.

At first, I don't mind them biting me, feeling they're too cute and too small to do me any harm, but with time the pain gets worse and becomes bothersome.

I start kicking with my feet, to get rid of the creatures, but they don't go away and continue biting with even greater vigor. I'm really beginning to hurt now, and kick real hard, and try brushing the creatures off with my hands, and scream, but they just won't go away.

The situation continues getting worse, and finally the pain becomes really bad, and so, desperate, I fill my lungs with air and roar as hard as I can, while continuing fighting, and then wake up.

I lay uncovered, having kicked off the comforter, which had slipped down to the floor, shivering from the cold.

One of the windows in the room was open and cold night mountain air was streaming inside. Streaming in with it were the sounds the vehicles of the retreating German army were making as they traveled down the highway.

Unexpectedly, a mournful whistle drowned out the other sounds—a train had just come out of the tunnel and was moving along the viaduct. The Germans were using all means possible to retreat.

*Stefa again?*

As I lay, slowly warming up, unable to fall asleep, I heard the door of Stefa's room open and father, walking once again on tiptoes, go back to his room, open the door, go inside, and close it.

# 5

---

*Your father went away?*

Next morning father got us all together and announced that he wouldn't be going back to his unit but would defect and join the partisans. The Russians were coming and we had to stand up against them to prevent them from killing more of us. Right now, members of the Ukrainian intelligentsia were being rounded up by the Russians in the areas they'd just occupied and their future was in danger. Measures had to be taken to prevent this. The primary reason he himself had joined the Germans was to acquire military training and experience. He had gotten that and was going now to put it to good use. He would be leaving that afternoon.

We should all leave as soon as possible because the Russians could overrun our region in a matter of days if not hours. They would know who he was—someone in town would surely tell them—and we would pay dearly for that. At the least we would be sent to Siberia, and might possibly suffer even worse fate.

The most endangered were Nora and me. Grandmother would likely not be bothered, and, besides, she was far advanced in years and it would be difficult for her to go into exile.

He had spoken to Stefa and she agreed to go with us. She would take her son along and would treat us as if we were her children. If nothing more, she was, after all, part of the family.

*He spoke to you?*

Nora's reaction was tears and pleading for him not to go. Mother had died and we were being left orphans. His explaining that regardless of whether he went back to his unit or joined the partisans, he would have to leave us alone didn't help. Neither did his pointing out that he couldn't simply desert and go with us to Germany—he would be caught and executed if he did that. Crying hysterically, she ran to her room and locked herself inside there.

Father took me with him into the room where the three of us used to sleep and talked to me.

I was standing up and he got down on one knee, put both of his arms on my shoulders, and, looking into my eyes, spoke.

He reminded me of the story of Agamemnon and his daughter Iphigenia we had discussed while I was reading *The Iliad* for the first time. Agamemnon sacrificed his daughter for the good of the people he led. A leader's obligation to his people comes before that to his family. He reminded me that I had agreed to that then, and I confirmed that, as well as that I did now too.

He said that he'd been asked to lead a battalion that was being formed just then and that he had agreed to do it. They needed him and he couldn't turn his back on them. It was his duty. He was sure the Russians would lose in the end—either by being defeated by the Germans or by their current allies in the West. He would be constantly thinking of us and somehow try to keep in touch, and was sure we would be reunited in the end.

He asked me to stay strong and watch over the others. It was my obligation as a man to do that. I was still a boy, but a boy is also a man.

Tears welled up in my eyes and, crying, I said that I would do as he asked but that I would prefer to go with him and be his *džura*, like older Cossacks used to have. I would assist him in everything, and would learn about fighting, and serve our people with him.

His eyes sparkling in a different way, he leaned forward, hugged me, and said he loved me more than anything else in the world but that such a thing was impossible. *Džuras* didn't exist anymore and it would be against the rules to try something like that. I must do as he asked me, stay firm, and not lose faith. The war would be over, we would be reunited, and everything would be fine again.

I agreed that he was right, and said that I would do as he had asked, but, hard as I tried, couldn't stop crying, and threw my arms around his neck, and hugged him as tight as I could in turn, and kissed his eyes and cheeks.

He kissed me back on eyes and cheeks and we stayed like this, hugging each other for a long time.

*He went away?*

He wore his military breeches and boots in addition to his regular shirt and jacket, taking along his belt with the pistol and the submachine gun and a small suitcase with personal items and pictures of mother, Nora, me, and the four of us together. (He didn't carry any grenades when he came home.) His army cap, shirt, and jacket, he asked to be burned and the ashes dispersed or buried.

He was meeting someone on the road to the village whose name I had heard while listening in to the conversation through the door. I asked to let me accompany him there but he said that was prohibited. He hugged and kissed us all and walked out the door. I saw him go down the path through the garden, pass through the gate, close it, turn right, and walk in the direction of the edge of town.

Suddenly, realizing I could do this, I ran into the room we'd talked in earlier, climbed out the window I had climbed in through when mother died, ran into the garden, climbed over the fence, and hiding behind other fences, bushes, and trees, watched him walk down the road that led into the hills.

For a while I lost sight of him, but after climbing the big hill he had to climb on the other side, I saw him again walking fast down the road, which soon joined a bigger one that led to the particular village, which he took. I had a good view of him now, and hiding behind bushes and trees, running from time to time while bent down low, I followed him for a long time until finally, lying in tall, seared grass which I was spreading with my hands, I saw him walk up to a wagon drawn by a horse, with a driver sitting up front, that'd been waiting there.

There was a man standing next to the wagon, he and the man shook hands, they climbed into the wagon, the driver cracked his whip, the wagon rolled forward, and in a few minutes disappeared behind the edge of the hill, where the road dipped. I didn't try running after it to see it a while longer.

As I was nearing home, while still quite a distance away, I could hear Nora's exceptionally furious banging away at the piano, erasing the images in my eyes.

# 6

_____

*The Germans left the house?*

Soon after I came home, an acquaintance of grandmother who lived on the street where our own house stood came running and informed us that the Germans that had lived there had just moved out. A truck and a couple of passenger cars drove up late that morning, some furniture and a whole bunch of other things were taken out, loaded into the vehicles, and they all drove away, leaving the house empty.

*You went to see it?*

I wanted for all of us to go there immediately and check it out, but grandmother and Stefa were reluctant to do it, fearing it was illegal, and I didn't even bother asking Nora, as she continued hammering away at the piano, oblivious of the world around her.

Fearing that the door was locked, I got the key to it father had held on to, which he kept in the drawer of the night table on his side of the bed, once again climbed out the window, and ran to the house.

Yuriy Tarnawsky

To my surprise the door was open, although the key I had brought did fit it.

With my heart once again in my throat, I went inside, closed the door, and walked from room to room.

The house was largely empty, with some things scattered on the floor and an occasional odd piece of furniture here and there.  These were mostly big items, such as wardrobes and beds, which would have been hard to take away.

The place looked strange at first, as if it belonged to someone else rather than us, but with time I began to recall the layout of the rooms I had noted while going through the house with my parents as it was being built, and I began to feel more and more that I was in my own—our—home.  With that realization, I began to see the beauty of the place—the high ceilings, the shiny parquet floors, the tall windows with clear glass panes unbroken by ribbings, the smooth, white enameled railings along the terrace by the side door on the main floor and the small balcony on the third....  The huge living room on the main floor could be divided in two by a movable folding wall made of shiny blond wood of the same kind as parquet of the floors.  I recalled father and mother talking about it and being unable to quite visualize it, and now I was seeing it!  The wall was folded and I proceeded to open it, to see how it changed the room.  I liked it better undivided, and closed the wall again. There was a mess in the kitchen, which bothered me, and so I started to clean it up, throwing some things into a garbage can and putting away others in drawers and closets. The floor was dirty, there was a broom, I picked it up, and swept the floor. I swept the floors in all the rooms on the main floor, but left those on the other two alone. It would have taken me too long.

A couple of the beds had sheets one them, and I straightened them out, making them look made up.

The bed in the big—my parents'—bedroom had a red satin sheet over it and I smoothed it out so that it shone like liquid red paint. I threw myself down onto the bed, bounced on it a few times, and decided I'd spend the night there, but then realized that I couldn't do it—they'd be worrying where I was and would come looking for me. I had promised father to behave and had to keep my word.

I took one more look at everything before leaving. The place belonged to us. I imagined the four of us living there, as if mother were still alive, father was with us, there was no war, and Nora and I weren't going away. Satiated and peaceful inside as I hadn't been for months, I went out, locked the door, put the key in my pocket, and went back to grandmother's. Once there, I put the key back in the night table drawer, where it'd been.

*You had a dream?*

I dreamed that night that I was staying alone in our house, and went out on the balcony, and there were no buildings around except open fields, full of yellow flowers you could see in the dark, and the sky overhead was a deep black, but full of bright stars. My shirt was open on my chest and a balmy breeze was caressing my face, bringing with it the sweet smell of grasses.

# 7

___

*Preparations for going away?*

For a few days there was nothing at home but frantic activities connected with going away.

Loaves of bread were baked, cut up into slices, put back in the oven, turned into dry toast, and stuffed into sacks to be taken along. Apples and pears, some not quite ripe yet, were picked, cut up into slices, dried in a similar way, put each into a separate slipcase, and then into a sack. A couple of sacks of potatoes and a small one with carrots were added. Somebody was paid to kill a pig, sausages were made, smoked, wrapped into newspapers, stacked into a basket, and placed next to the other sacks with food.  Other provisions, such as jars of lard, salt, soap, etc. were added to the hoard.

Our clothes were readied and we each packed a suitcase with them as well as with personal items, such as a comb, toothbrush, towel, etc. I wanted to take the two volumes of Sven Hedin's books along, but they were too heavy and as I was looking through my little library huddling on the shelf, I finally settled on the slim dog-eared volume of *Axel's Cave*. It reminded me of the happiest years of my childhood, dealt with traveling, which is what I was undertaking, and there was something in it which seemed to suggest it was the book I should take along. Part of it must have been the dreams of dark nights I had been having, but there was something else I just couldn't put my finger on. It simply felt it was the right book for me to take.

Important documents, such as birth certificates and family photographs were collected, put into boxes and stored in one of two suitcases Stefa was to carry. Her son came to stay with us and we waited for the train that was to take us away to come.

*You boarded the train?*

We boarded the train in the middle of the night.

We knew it was coming, and I slept all dressed up while waiting for it, and shook all over on being woken up, my teeth chattering as if from being cold.

Grandmother smelled of the times prior to the war as I hugged her before walking out the door and left a big wet spot where she kissed me on my cheek. Dressed as always in black head to toe, she filled the doorway like a big conical mound of the ashes of my past watching us drive away in the wagon. It would have been hard to get past it.

The town was empty and dark as we drove through it, but the railroad station was bustling with people and was illuminated by the cold, harsh light of carbide lamps. Everyone was rushing this way and that and the trains stood patiently waiting on the tracks—a long row of red freight cars, their doors open, some filled with people staring out, others being boarded, still others caves of impenetrable darkness, waiting to be filled.

Someone had turned over a pail of wild strawberries one of the village women must have brought to sell from earlier that day, and it left a big spot of red slippery substance on the stone platform from being trampled by people's feet.

Some would slip on it, and I did too, and so fell down, and stained my leg and shorts red on one side, as if in a puddle of blood. Everyone said it was an omen of things to come. The leg I cleaned the next day when we stopped at a station and there was water to wash up, but it took Stefa a couple of tries to more or less wash away the stain on the shorts. Traces of it stayed on for good.

The four of us got into a car in which aunt Eda and uncle Genko were already waiting. There was room for it for a couple dozen people. We found a spot in one of the corners for ourselves and our things, spread out the bedclothes we had brought along, lay down, and waited for the train to drive off and for ourselves to go to sleep.

Yuriy Tarnawsky

After a long time, silently, as if in fear, without any hooting or whistle, it heaved, hesitated for a second or two, and laboriously rolled forward, gradually gaining speed, heading west, leaving the viaduct, town, and tunnel behind it.

It was still pitch-dark outside, and after a while I fell asleep, lulled by the train's rocking, clanking of the couplings that joined the cars, squeaking of springs, and clicking of the wheels on the rails.

# 8

_____

*How was the train ride?*

We made slow progress, sometimes stopping for a few minutes, at others—for hours, waiting for permission to proceed, be it on the main track or on a side one, shunted there to let other trains go by, usually those that carried German soldiers, such as I described earlier.

Once or twice a day the train would stop at a station where it was possible to get water, to wash up, and cook. The cooking was done out in the countryside, next to the track, where people were able to gather firewood for fires to cook on.

Stefa attended to that and I helped her by gathering sticks for the fire and stones to put the pot on, with Nora helping out or keeping an eye on Stefa's son. After a couple of stops, we settled on a few stones and carried them with us, so as use them the next time without having to look for new ones.

In spite of what the train ride really meant, I was excited about going away—I was traveling to a strange country and would be passing through all sorts of unknown regions, something that was not unlike what Sven Hedin had been doing, going down the Tarim River through Sinkiang.

The twisting and turning the train was making, in fact, made me think of the course of the Tarim river, as if I was traveling in a boat. It was also exciting to be able to see the two ends of the train—the smoke-belching engine up front and the end car in the back, as it was rounding a long curve. You could see then the whole train with the car doors open and people standing in them or sitting on the floor with their feet hanging out, exploring with their eyes the ever-changing landscape. I liked doing this in addition because it reminded me of how it was when we took the train to stay with grandmother during the summers when I was little, when it was rounding a curve, and it was as if I'd been transported for a brief moment back to those idyllic times when there was no war, and I hadn't experienced all those horrible things I'd been through since, and the four of us—father, mother, Nora, and I—lived, peaceful and happy, at hrabia Karol's estate.

*Train depot?*

After a couple of days, we arrived at a huge train depot in a Hungarian town and stayed there for a while.

There were many trains standing on the tracks with horse-drawn wagons between them that had brought those that were fleeing, and people were moving their belongings into rail cars. Most of the wagons and horses were abandoned at that point and were taken over by Hungarian authorities, although some were going back to where they'd come from, the drivers not having planned to flee but having been hired to bring those that were fleeing and drop them off.

The trains were shuffled and reshuffled, cars were added on and taken off them, new trains were formed, and some were sent off while others waited.

Among the mess of wagons, horses, and civilians, could be seen Hungarian gendarmes with black hats on their heads that had rooster feathers stuck rakishly on one side, walking around with a haughty expression on their faces. They looked forbidding and seemed out of place both in time and space, reminding me of pictures in books with stories dealing with forested mountainous regions, game wardens, hunters, and brigands. It seemed we were founding ourselves in some half-civilized setting a century or more earlier.

*Pan Atrament?*

I wandered around the tracks all day between the trains and wagons, not having anything to do. While doing this, I think on the third day after our arrival, I saw the figure of pan Atrament standing next to a wagon, gazing around inquisitively, as if searching for someone, looking lost and confused.

Yuriy Tarnawsky

As he saw me, his face lit up and he motioned frantically for me to come. He'd arrived a day earlier and had been planning to flee, but had a change of heart and decided to go back. To move to a foreign land at his age was too difficult and he wanted to return home. His belongings were already in the wagon and the driver was going to drive him back.

He had one concern however—he'd been working on a book called "Theory of Man," which he had just finished and in which he outlined what it meant to be a human being in our times, and he didn't want to take it with him. He would never be able to make it available to the public under the Russians. He wanted someone to take it with him to the West and have it published there.

I'd been heaven-sent to him! There was no better person who could have shown up at the moment. I was still a young boy, but I was smart and had a bright future. He would entrust the manuscript to me and was sure I would find a publisher for it.

Without waiting for my response, he delved into one of the bundles in the wagon, got out a thin packet of paper inside a folder tied together with a twine in the form of a cross, and thrust it in my hands.

I could read it, he said, and he was sure I would get a lot out of it. Since I had just lost my mother and home and since my father was away, it would help me to carry on. I was very advanced for my age, and from having observed me for a long time, he knew I would understand what he had written.

192

Surprised and overwhelmed, not knowing how to respond, I took the manuscript without saying a word and pressed it with both hands to my chest as I frequently did with books that I read as I carried them around. I didn't quite understand the nature of the mission I was committing to but was determined to carry it out the way I'd been asked.

*Amor?*

Did I know, he asked, changing the subject, that there'd been a great battle between Ukrainian partisans and the Russians a few days ago? He named the village near which the battle took place, which was the one the man that had visited my father that night had talked about. No, I couldn't, he concluded on his own. It happened the day before he left and everyone in town had been talking about it, but the train we were on departed before then. The Ukrainian partisans were fighting the Russian, he went on, and had had the upper hand, but then the Russian army broke through and surrounded the Ukrainians. The unit was annihilated. Many were killed and taken prisoner. Only a few managed to escape. The unit was led by a commander called "Amor."

I was stumped for a second by the name "Amor" and didn't respond. It sounded familiar to me, but I couldn't tell why. But then the name of father's horse at hrabia Karol's estate "Jan Amor" came back to me and I realized what it most likely meant. Father had dropped "Jan," which was Polish for "John," and retained "Amor." "Amor" meant "love" in Latin, and knowing father, he might have felt it was an appropriate pseudonym for him.

With my heart practically in my throat, I asked what happened to the commander. Was he killed or captured, or did he escape?

Pan Atrament didn't know the answer to that. Not much was known about the battle and all sorts of rumors were circulated, but nobody said anything about Amor.

I breathed easier but didn't let on what I was feeling. I preferred not to tell him what I had thought. It was as if I'd eliminate or at least reduce the possibility that something bad had happened to my father.

Eager to get away from the source of the bad news, once again as if thinking this would make them less likely to be true, I said that I had to go and that I would do everything possible to have the manuscript published, and we said good-bye.

As I was leaving, he mentioned with sadness in his voice that Obscura died the night before he left. She'd sensed he was going away and decided to depart herself. They'd meet in the other world. He didn't have time to bury her and asked neighbors to do it. If they hadn't done it, he might still be able to do it if he came home right away.

*Nora?*

The situation in the rail car was charged. They'd also learned about the battle and the commander Amor, and everyone was upset. Aunt Eda was paler than ever, uncle Genko looked more morose than usual, and Stefa's eyes were red. It was clear she'd been crying. Nora was hysterical. She kept screaming through tears that Amor must have been father, because father had a horse named "Jan Amor," which he loved, and that, needing a pseudonym, he selected "Amor" because "Jan" was a Polish name, and he didn't want to be thought of as a Pole, being the commander of a Ukrainian partisan unit. She was sure that father had been killed, and now we were orphans, with nobody to take care of us.

Something seemed to snap inside me and I was overtaken by an uncontrollable anger. I ran up to her and, red in the face, screamed at her that that wasn't true. Father was an exemplary soldier and he wouldn't have let Russians kill him. He'd escaped out of the encirclement just a while ago unharmed, and would have done it this time. Besides, the partisans needed him and would have done everything possible to protect him. He must have gotten away!

Then, without having planned to say this, and actually believing my words, as if they were true, I said that I'd just spoken to pan Atrament, and he had told me about the battle, and said that father did get away. People had seen him after the battle with some of his men, and they were regrouping, and waiting for reinforcements, and were going to fight on.

A huge stone seemed to have shifted off my soul which I realized now had been pressing down on it. The world suddenly looked brighter, as did life and my future in it. I felt better than I had before hearing the news from pan Atrament, perhaps as well as before the war, when the four of us were together. Father was alive and well, and he would fight for our people, and be victorious, and one day the three of us would be together again.

As if exhausted by an enormous effort I hadn't been up to, I sat down on the floor where I stood, covered my face with my hands, and cried, shaking with sobs.

Someone's hands embraced me, and pressed me to a warm body, and I saw it was Stefa, who had kneeled down beside me. She bent down and kissed me first on the cheeks, and then the eyes, and held me tight for a long time, stroking my hair.

I didn't see Nora at first, but then noticed she was there before me, kneeling down on the floor and hammering away furiously at it as if it were the keyboard of a piano. This was something she would do often from then on.

# 9

---

*Theory of Man?*

Our train left the next day and I read pan Atrament's manuscript sitting on the floor at the door, with my legs dangling over edge. A rope had been strung across the opening, to prevent people from falling out, although it wasn't thick enough to do that. It served no more than a reminder there was danger beyond it.

The track ran through a flat landscape, with neat white-walled homes under red-tiled roofs surrounded by picket fences, amid fruit trees and shrubbery close to the track, followed by well-cultivated fields that stretched all the way to soft low hills on the horizon. Some of the former were already bare, but others still bulged with dark green vegetation which waited to be harvested. High up above the land, not obtruding it, hung a cloudless pale blue sky, with the sun in the middle. The air was fresh and cool as if at the beginning of summer. The climate here seemed milder and wetter than on the other side of the mountains.

I took off the string with which the folder was tied and stared looking through the manuscript. It was surprisingly thin, no more than twenty pages, and was written in black ink in pan Atrament's neat calligraphic hand. It looked almost as if it'd been printed in beautiful cursive font. The text started after the title page.

The first sentence I read surprised me—it was "In the beginning God created the heaven and the earth,"—exactly as the opening in the Bible, which I remembered from having memorized it in school in the class on catechism. I read on, and the text continued the same way— "And the earth was without shape and empty; and there was darkness on the surface of oceans. And the spirit of God moved on the surface of the waters...."

I was stunned—was this a joke? Did pan Armament pull my leg by ironically suggesting that I should look for solace from my plight in the Bible, to discover that I couldn't find it there?

It didn't make sense. He sounded serious and couldn't have made light of my situation.

Reluctant to proceed, but not giving up, I read on and saw what he had done—he had merged some Bible text with his own words, modifying the meaning of the former and channeling it in a different direction. This became apparent when he introduced the figure of man. His text read, "And God said, let us make man in his neighbor's image, after his neighbor's likeness," instead of, "And God said, let us make man in my own image, after my own likeness," and further along, "And God made man from the dust on the ground, and breathed into him the breath of life and his own spirit; and man became a living creature with God's spirit in him," instead of "And God made man from the dust on the ground, and breathed into him the breath of life; and man became a living soul." He was saying that all men were created the same, and all had something of the divine in them.

Knowing what I'd learned in my short life about man, I felt this was silly and was ready to stop reading, but curious where he was going to wind up, read on, finding his writing gradually not so much silly as boring, and so stated skipping first sentences, then paragraphs, and finally pages. He was peddling the idea that all men were good, and all had the divine spirit in them, and that mankind was the embodiment of God. I hadn't come yet to the end, but it was clear where he was going to end up—men should love and worship each other as God, as they had once loved and worshipped God alone.

I had been putting the pages I'd looked through on the floor next to me. A gust of wind suddenly blew in from the outside and carried the top page away. It rose up like a white bird into the air, fluttered in it gracefully for a few seconds, and vanished, descending on my right. The train was moving to the left.

This made me think of how petals are plucked off daisies while one says "She loves me/She loves me not." I found this amusing and decided to mimic it with the pages of the manuscript—I'd toss them out one by one in the air, while saying "God loves me/God loves me not." It'd be interesting where I wind up.

I picked up the pages I'd laid down on the floor next to me and, starting with the first one and proceeding sequentially, began to throw them one by one into the air while calling out loud the phrases.

Uncle Genko was apparently watching me and after I threw out a few pages yelled at me not to do it. I was littering the landscape with paper.

I replied that it wasn't paper but daisy petals and that I was trying to find out whether God loves me or not.

I don't know if he heard what I said, but he immediately bellowed in an angry voice for me to stop.

We were crossing a river just then, going over a bridge, and not so much out of fear of him, as in a spirit of merriment, I threw the whole stack of paper in the air and saw it flutter like a flock of scared-off pigeons before descending into the water, screaming out loud, "God loves me not!"

I turned my head in his direction and shouted arrogantly that I wasn't littering the landscape—the pages would fall into the water which would carry them away.

He was glaring at me menacingly out of the darkness with his crazed eyes.

*You had a dream?*

That night I had a dream about my father and mother dancing away in the night.  It was the last dream of this kind I ever had.

It's at night, and I'm standing in a field exactly like the one I saw in the dream I had after the visit to our home.  The earth is empty and flat, but curves down on the horizon and is overgrown with big yellow flowers that shine like the stars in the black sky above. There's no moon, but I can see perfectly clearly all around.  It seems this time it's not only because of the stars, but also the flowers. They emit light like the stars.

Suddenly, I feel something like a gust of wind blow past me, and when I look around, I see that it was father and mother dancing together.  They seemed to have gone through me like a puff of air.

Mother is dressed in the long black dress she was buried in, and I can see the rhinestone brooch sparkle on her chest. Father is wearing the clothes he was in while going away.  He has his submachine gun with him and you can see the strap it

Yuriy Tarnawsky

hangs on across the back of his neck.  It must make it uncomfortable for mother, for she's leaning away more than one would expect.  Still, she dances on, bearing the discomfort, as I did when he held me up on coming from the front, clearly enjoying what the two of them are doing.

The dancing they used to do when I was little was different—slower and more complicated—most likely tangos.  This one is faster and consists exclusively of twirling—probably a waltz.

They hold tightly onto each other, staring into their partner's eyes, drunk with the dancing, oblivious of everything around them. As they twirl, they get farther and farther away from me and closer and closer to the horizon.

And now the earth is not overgrown with flowers any more but is smooth and shiny like a dance floor, with the stars in the sky reflected in it, which seem to have taken over the place of the flowers.

The two keep twirling along it, getting smaller and smaller and sinking gradually more and more into the ground as they near the horizon.

A thought passes through my mind that I should run after them, to see them longer, but I suppress it.  There's no point in doing it.  They'll disappear anyway.

A little longer, and they vanish from my sight.

# 10

---

*The train ride?*

We were told the train was heading for Austria and therefore could have gotten there in a day, but there was more important traffic going in that direction and we were forced to take all sorts of circuitous routes and waited in some desolate spots for days. In addition to Hungary, we passed for brief stretches through Slovakia and Czechia, and I believe once through Romania. In Czechia people would ask us *"Prečo utíkáte?"*—"Why are you fleeing?" and when we explained it was from the Russians, they scoffed at us. They said Russians were good.

*Food?*

Food was prepared when the train had stopped and we were told we'd rest there for a while. As I explained earlier, people would gather twigs, and dry weeds, and whatever else that burned, build fires next to the track, and prepare food. For us, as I have also said, it was Stefa who did the cooking. Usually, she'd prepare some kind of soup, containing potatoes, and vegetables—mostly carrots—and perhaps meat. If the train signaled that it was leaving, the cooking was abandoned, pots with the half-cooked meals were grabbed, and quickly gotten to the car.

After a while, the provisions we'd brought along began to spoil—potatoes and carrots grew soft and sprouted shoots, weevils appeared in the toast, and sausages turned slimy. Some people had them suspended on strings from the roof of the car, and they hung there big and shiny, swaying back and forth as the train moved, like penises of horses that'd just urinated.

*Air raid?*

While stationed once in the train depot in a big Hungarian town, I experienced my first air raid. It was in the middle of the night and I was shaken out of sleep by Stefa to the ear-piercing sound of sirens wailing. I'd never heard them before and thought it was people screaming like that in fear, or perhaps bombs already falling, but she told me it was sirens and explained what they were. Shaking all over, in near total darkness, barely able to tie my shoe laces, I dressed and ran out with everyone into the field, away from the station, but the town wasn't bombed that night.

Once we got back to the rail car, I thought what we'd been through was fun and looked forward to another air raid soon. It was amusing to see how some adults were afraid of what might happen to them—turning pale, and crying, and shaking all over, and trying to hide. I had no fear whatsoever and was sure nothing could happen to me.

Worst of all was aunt Eda—her face had turned white as chalk, her teeth chattered, her hands jumped all over, and when she sat still, her feet rattled on the ground like someone's nervous fingers tapping out a wild rhythm. It took her a long time to get back to normal.

# 11

---

*Stefa?*

It was clear Stefa was fond of me. She helped me wash and dress, and made sure my hair was properly combed, which she did often, since I didn't bring along my own mirror and it was hard to borrow someone else's. I usually stayed around her when she cooked, not so much to talk, as to be next to her to feel her spiritual warmth, as I felt the physical warmth of the fire. Sometimes, as she hugged her son, she'd hug me too, pressing both of us to her body, while gently rocking.

She said I looked a lot like my father and that I would grow up to be as strong and handsome as he.

When she'd kiss me, it was often on the eyes, which she said were beautiful.

*Nora?*

At one point Nora began to ignore us. She did eat with us most of the time and occasionally interacted, but moved her sleeping things next to those of a Polish family which came from our town and stayed almost exclusively with them, interacting in Polish. Sometimes she even shared their food.

I found this upsetting and at one point asked her what was the matter. Why did she act like that?

She looked at me angrily and said in Polish, *"Zostaw mnie. Co chcesz ode mnie?"*—"Leave me alone. What do you want from me?"

I was stunned. We'd never spoken among ourselves in Polish when alone, not even when we lived in Poland, and I burst out in anger in Ukrainian, turning red in the face, *"Zradnycja! Pol'koju-s' stala, todi, jak tato za nas vojuje!"*—"Traitor! You've turned Polish, while father is fighting for us!"

She looked with hatred into my eyes and said in a contemptuous voice, once again in Polish, *"Kłamałeś mnie wtedy. Ojca już nie ma."*—"You lied to me then. Father's no longer alive."

Shocked to the limit, speechless, unable to find words with which to reply her, I watched her turn around, walk away, and sit down satisfied next to her newly found family.

*Uncle Genko?*

Yuriy Tarnawsky

It was shortly thereafter that the following happened.

The train had stopped at some sidetrack in the country and we waited for permission to proceed. Most of the people in the car had gone outside, while I and a few others remained.

The Polish family I mentioned above had brought along a big illustrated Bible they'd read sometimes in. I had been watching them do it with envy, but was too shy to ask them to let me see it. Besides, I didn't want to do it because of what was happening between Nora and them.

I saw it now lying on top of one of their bundles and thought I'd take a quick look at it. I was curious what the illustrations in it were like.

Uncle Genko saw me do it and bellowed in his bull's voice for me to put it down. It wasn't mine and I had no right to touch it.

I said I'd just take a quick look at the pictures in it and would put it right back, but he bellowed once again for me to put the book down.

I'm not sure if I was going to do it or not because at that instant he ran up to me, tore the book out of my hands, threw it back onto the bundle, grabbed me by the collar of my shirt in the back, turned me around, and began hitting me with the palm of his hand on my behind.

I had never been spanked in my life, and a feeling of outrage I had never experienced before welled up in me, and I screamed at the top of my voice for him to stop, and wiggled around so that it was hard for him to go on hitting me.

Hearing my screaming, people came rushing back to the car, the two of us were separated, and both he and I explained what had happened.

The Polish people said I'd done nothing wrong and that I could look at the Bible as much as I wanted, but uncle Genko said that I was an unruly boy and that before dying, mother had asked him to watch over me, and that that was what he was doing now.

Trembling all over and, as I felt, white in the face, but otherwise strangely calm, I said to him in near-whisper through my teeth, while boring with my eyes into his, that I was going to kill him for what he'd done, and that he wasn't going to do this to me ever again.

He smiled in an embarrassed way, shifted his eyes aside, turned around, and, clearly defeated, walked away.

# 12

---

*Your revenge?*

A couple of days later our train was stopped in the middle of the day and ordered to stay on the track to wait for permission to proceed. It was expected we'd be moving soon.

Aware of that, nobody tried do any cooking and most people stayed in their cars or, if they got out, moved about close to them.

It must have been near some large city because there were three or four tracks running close to each other and trains were going up and down along them constantly, all moving very fast.

I had stayed in the car and lay on my back on my bedding, as I recall, looking at the ceiling, involved in one of my imaginary exploits.

My thoughts were suddenly interrupted by all sorts of screams and running back and forth coming from the outside. Intrigued, I quickly got up and jumped out of the car.

There was hardly anybody on the side of the train I was on, but something really serious seemed to be happening on the other.

I crawled quickly under the couplings between our car and the next to the other side and pushed my way into a group of people gathered in one spot not far away.

Lying face down on the ground next to the track on the left was the figure of a man. His arms and legs were stretched out peacefully along his body, as if he was resting, but much of his skull on the left was gone. In place of it was mostly nothing, but also lots of blood mixed with something gray, looking like thick oatmeal. The hair on what was left of his head was matted with blood and the gray matter too, and there was blood and the gray matter on his back and shoulders and all around him on the ground.

For a few seconds I was left unmoved, thinking it was some strange person I had never seen before, but then I noticed something disturbing—the blue checkered shirt and black pants the man wore seemed familiar.... They looked like those worn by uncle Genko!

My heart sank. Yes! It was he! Those were his clothes, and his dark curly hair, and the burly upper body, and the powerful arms and legs, and the big lump on the back of his neck! He'd been killed! I said I was going to kill him, and I had done it! The fact that I'd been lying on my back in the car while this happened didn't change things. It was my wish to kill him that had led to his death. I was guilty of it and would be punished!

From the jumbled fragments of what people were saying, it appeared that he'd been strolling between the two tracks and was hit by a fast-moving train that'd just passed by. He'd been walking in the same direction as the train, and turned around abruptly with his head bent down, as was his custom, and went with it into the side of the engine. It seemed he didn't hear the train coming.

Terrified, I was going to run away and hide someplace, but virtually all the people gathered around me were strangers, and nobody paid attention to me, and I was curious what was going to happen next, so I stayed on. I would worry about what would be done to me afterwards.

Inquiries were made who he was, and aunt Eda was brought along, but after recognizing the body, she refused to do anything. When asked what should be done, she said she didn't know. When it was suggested she stay with the body to see it properly buried, she fell into hysterics, cried and screamed she wouldn't stay behind to be killed by the Russians, ran off to the car, and hid there in the corner, among their common belongings. She stayed there from then on practically all the time.

While people debated what to do—notify those in charge of the train? take the body along? bury it right there?—a signal was heard from the engine up front that we were leaving.  His body was quickly moved to the middle between the two tracks, the blanket he'd been sleeping under was fetched, and the body was covered with it, with its edges tucked under, so that it wouldn't be blown away by wind.  They tried to get his identification papers to put them on him, but nobody knew where they were, so he was left unidentified.

In the car, nobody accused me of having anything to do with his being killed.  They'd either forgotten what I'd said, hadn't taken it seriously, thought I'd merely warned him not to hit me again, or hadn't heard it at all.

# 13

------

*Stefa's son?*

Another couple of days later I woke up in the middle of the night. It was pitch-dark in the car and the train wasn't moving. We'd been traveling when I was falling asleep, but had stopped and were apparently waiting once again for permission to proceed. It was probably the train's stopping that had woken me up.

It appeared we were somewhere out in the country, for it was still all around. Everyone seemed asleep. The only thing that could be heard was people's heavy breathing.

The preceding day Stefa had spent a lot of time with her son and had paid no attention to me. That'd bothered me at first, but I'd managed to push it out of my mind and went on with whatever I was doing. Now however, the feeling came back to me even clearer than before. It was a fear of being abandoned. She was the only one I had left and if she were to turn her back on me, I'd be completely alone. The sensation was extremely uncomfortable, as if I were finding myself in a very tight place which was making me feel claustrophobic. The back of my head and the nape of my neck tingled, as if growing numb. I had to do something!

We all slept on the floor, with Stefa's son on my left and she beyond him. I could hear his soft breathing with a slight rattle in it as if he had a mild cold. I had threatened to kill uncle Genko, succeeded in doing it, and had gotten away without being punished. What if I killed Stefa's son? I could pinch his nose, preventing him from breathing, and he would suffocate. Nobody would know it was I who killed him and Stefa would then have only me to love. Besides, what was the point of his living on? Stefa had a hard time to get proper food for him— milk and eggs—and what we all ate was making him weak and sick. And if he were to survive, what would await him?—Life in a strange country, among hostile people.... And if his mother died, what would he do? He was better off dying now.

I was lying on my back, so, holding my breath, I rolled over onto my left side, stretched out my right hand, found his nose with my fingers, and pinched it together. It was tiny, and its nostrils were hard, as if made from rubber, and would open right up as soon as I relaxed my fingers. They reminded me of a rubber duck I used to play with in the water when I was taking a bath as a small child.

Oddly enough, he didn't try to take my hand away however, or wiggle out from under it, but merely started crying. At first it was just a whimper, but soon it turned into loud cries.

For an instant, I thought of covering his mouth with my hand, to suffocate him, but realized it wouldn't work, and besides heard Stefa stirring on the other side. What would happen if she found my hand over her son's mouth?!

Turning cold with fear, I quickly moved my hand away, just in time to avoid being touched by hers, with which she was reaching for his face.

Hoping with all my might she wouldn't guess what had happened, I rolled into a ball under my covers, trying to get as small as possible, and lay dead still, waiting for what might come. My original instinct was to roll over onto the other side but I decided against it. It was better not to move. Rolling over might bring me to her attention.

She didn't suspect anything and after quieting her son went back to sleep. Relieved, I relaxed, and when the train began moving, fell asleep after a while, once again lulled by its rocking and the sounds it made.

# 14

---

*A Hungarian town?*

It was Sunday morning, and we had stopped on a track close to some small Hungarian town. We were told we'd stay there until afternoon, and a lot of people decided to go into town in the morning to explore it. I went along.

The place looked beautiful, with neat white-walled homes under red-tiled roofs behind picket fences, such as I'd seen throughout the country from the train, and clean, cobblestoned streets with carefully pruned trees along them. It was the prettiest town I'd ever seen.

Especially beautiful was the central square, which sloped downward from the railroad station, from the direction of which we were coming. It was large and rectangular, surrounded by similar-looking two-storied buildings, once again with white walls and red-tiled roofs, with a much larger, three-storied city hall at the end, above the red-tiled roof of which rose a tall and thin green metal spire with a weathervane on top. A well-maintained sidewalk of big stone plates ran alongside the buildings, separated on all three sides from the open area in the center by a cobblestoned road. The central part was paved with the same stone plates as the sidewalk and was surrounded by a dense row of trees, whose crowns were pruned into spheres that didn't quite touch. Long white benches with curving backs made of thin wooden slats, similar to the one in front of the building we lived in at hrabia Karol's estate, were situated at regular intervals under the trees.

I liked the combination of the colors—red, white, and green, and only later realized they were the colors of the Hungarian national flag.  I don't know whether this was planned or coincidental.

*A market hall?*

One of the buildings on the right turned out to be a market hall, and we went into it after walking around the square for a while.

Markets in our town were held in the open, with wagons, stalls, tables, and provisions laid out on the ground all intermixed, and this was the first enclosed one I saw.

There were all sorts of wares on display, ranging from clothing, through cookware, to food, with everything being neatly arranged, and we strolled through the aisles, gazing around in admiration, astounded by such abundance and order.

Most astounding was food, of which there was plenty—huge round loaves of white bread the size of pillows, some untouched, others sliced into halves or quarters, stacked up on tables, sausages of different shapes and sizes suspended on racks like musical instruments, huge wheels of cheese, some whole, others with wedges cut out, thick slabs of white pork belly with a layer of red paprika on top laid out flat like bedding, and so on, and so forth, and lots and lots of fruit.

It was this that attracted me the most. We'd traveled now for weeks and ate mostly what we'd brought along, and I hadn't had anything fresh since leaving home. Most alluring were watermelons. They were small and round, with green and white stripped skin and bright red fiery insides. I had forgotten the disgust I'd felt at being forced by mother to finish eating the slice of watermelon she'd bitten into and couldn't take my eyes off them. My mouth kept filling up with saliva and I had to swallow it as if drinking water from a glass. There were little triangular pieces of watermelon cut for customers to taste before deciding whether or not to buy, and some people were taking these, but I was reluctant to do the same, since I felt it was clear I had no money to spend.

On one table there were apples, and pears, and apricots, and plums, and fruit the size of apples, but fuzzy on the outside like apricots, and they attracted me the most. They were peaches, but I didn't know that since they didn't grow on the other side of the mountains, and I'd never seen them before. I thought they were a special kind of apple. A bunch of people who were buying something were shielding me from the owner on the other side of the table, and I realized that I could take one of these, put it in my pocket, and simply walk away. With my heart in my throat once again, I reached with my hand for the closest one, took it in my fingers, and felt its roundness and fuzz under my palm as if already tasting it. Nobody was saying anything and all I had to do was to put it in my pocket and go away.

But at that instant the image of my father appeared in my mind and I remembered who I was. I recalled how I used to steel myself against the hardships that life was going bring me when we lived at hrabia Karol's estate, in particular how easily I overcame my hunger and gladly accepted the punishment of having to skip suppers for destroying my sister's doll. Was I not able to resist the temptation to taste a piece of some exotic fruit right now? And what would father and mother and especially other people who knew me think of me if they saw me stealing? I cringed at the thought of them seeing me even contemplating such an act and wished I could hide someplace and never come out again. I couldn't do it!

A different person now, all bright inside like a room filled with light the shutters in which have suddenly been flung open, I put the piece of fruit down on the pile, turned around, and proudly walked away.

*A Hungarian woman?*

Seemingly towering over my surroundings now, as if viewing everything from high above, I strolled through the aisles between the table, no longer craving or even admiring what I saw, but merely noting it and storing away in my memory.

At one point, while doing this, I saw a few paces before me a couple, clearly locals, a middle-aged man and a somewhat younger woman, walking in my direction. They were both neatly dressed, the man in a dark suit with shirt and tie, and the woman in a light flowery dress and high heels, probably having just come out of the church. The man was average-looking, but the woman was extremely beautiful, with a classical face like a glass of clear water and luminous eyes that reminded me of pani Afrodyta's.

She'd been looking away when I first saw her, but then shifted her eyes onto me, looked into mine, and after a slight hesitation, smiled—she noticed my eyes too and found them beautiful. Had I been my father, she would have been ready to become my lover!

I smiled back at her, and we walked past each other as if nothing had happened, her husband not having noticed anything.

Elated, having lost all interest in the things around me, I quickly walked out of the market place and headed back to the train. I couldn't remember when I'd felt this good last time.

# 15

___

*In the reeds?*

Stefa had prepared lunch, but I didn't feel like eating and decided to explore the area around the track. We still had a couple of hours before we left, so I had plenty of time to do it. There was something that looked like a small lake or a large pond nearby and some people had gone there to investigate, and I decided to have a look myself.

It appeared to be a lake rather than a pond because it was irregularly shaped and part of it had gone dry and was overgrown with reeds. They were tall, probably over two meters high, and grew thick, so that it was hard to move through them.

I found this a challenge, and set off in one direction, pushing my way through the thicket by trampling the stalks down with my feet and pushing them out of the way with my hands and elbows.

Having gotten deep inside, I stopped and decided to stay there. It was nice and cozy being surrounded on all sides by tall slender stalks, as if by a wall, and to be able to see the blue sky with the little puffs of white clouds drifting through it between the feathery tips of the reeds high up. I hadn't been alone since leaving home and was overjoyed to be able to do it.

The ground under my feet was wet, but I was able to shape a kind of bed out of the reeds around me by bending and trampling them down, lay down on it, made myself comfortable, and looked at the sky.

There were people all around me and I could hear them walking around and talking, but I was all alone in my little enclosure and could do as I pleased.

I imagined myself in Egypt, someplace on the Nile, like where Moses was when his mother had put him in a basket, or in India, with tigers crawling through tall grass, stalking their prey, and also in the *plavni* wetlands along the Dnipro River with the Zaporizhian Cossacks, as they prepared themselves to go on an expedition against the Turks, readying their swift low *čajka* boats. I remembered what great fighters they were and how they would hide under water from Turks and Tatars by submerging themselves fully while breathing through a reed, to emerge in time to fight the enemy and win. I wished I could try this there myself.

Yuriy Tarnawsky

*Quiet all around?*

I must have stayed there daydreaming for half an hour or more, when I realized that it was quiet all around.

At first this didn't bother me, but then the realization of what it might mean sunk into my consciousness and I turned cold. Was everyone gone because the train had left? I seemed to remember hearing a while back the sound of the train hooting, signaling it was about to leave. I also seemed to remember hearing then people shouting to each other and scrambling to get out of the reeds.

Yes, I concluded, I was sure now I did hear the train whistle blowing, warning everyone to return, and that people had been rushing away to get to it in time. It was a while ago— five minutes or more. And I had ignored it!

*You ran?*

Like possessed, I jumped up and tried to run through the reeds, following the path I'd made earlier. It was impossible to do it, and my progress was more of a struggle of freeing myself from someone's clutches than a run. I kept pushing aside the accursed reeds that were getting in my way, and stumbling, and falling, and rising again, to repeat the same all over.

But eventually I found myself in the open and saw in the distance high up on the embankment above me the train. It was moving already, although still slowly, and I could see the dark figures of perhaps half a dozen persons running after it, trying to catch it.

*You shouted?*

Desperate, I shouted for them to halt the train, stretched out my hand, stumbled, fell, got up, and ran again, reaching out from time to time with my hand as though this would help. But the train kept moving faster and faster, growing smaller and smaller every second. I couldn't tell if all the people that were trying to catch it had managed to do it, but I no longer saw anyone. I hoped I was wrong and that at least one of them hadn't managed to get on, so that I wouldn't be left alone.

*You ran on?*

I continued running however. Only the tops of the last few cars of the train could still be seen now, but I thought there may still be a chance I could catch it. Perhaps someone would manage to notify the engineer there was a person being left behind and he would stop.

I remembered then the instant on the hospital train when I had tarried on it and nearly didn't get off, when I told myself I would never do anything so stupid again. I had done something much more stupid now! But I pushed the thought out of my mind. Now was not the time to dwell on my stupidity. I had to catch the train! And so, I ran on.

Yuriy Tarnawsky

*You got to the track?*

No longer checking whether the train was still there or not, but looking all the time under my feet to make sure I wouldn't fall down and waste time, I reached the embankment, climbed it, and stopped.

The train was gone. I could still see it, though, on the track, way in the distance, getting smaller and smaller, as if trying to turn into the vanishing point in a perspective drawing. The land was flat and empty on both sides of it, with a huge empty sky above. I looked around and didn't see anybody. All the people who were trying to get onto the train had made it. I was alone.

*You remembered?*

I remembered how people had said my falling down and staining my leg and shorts on the spilled wild strawberries was an omen of things to come. They were right. This is what was going to happen to me on the trip. It was predestined from the beginning. Ironically, I was wearing these shorts at the moment and there were traces of the stain left on them even now. More bad things were in store for me I would have to face.

*You understood?*

And now I understood why I felt *Axel's Cave* was the right book to take with me when I was leaving home—it was because my trip would lead to loneliness.

*You also remembered?*

I also remembered the kittens I'd drowned on the bridge over the Vechir and thought how cruel I'd been to them. Was I now being punished for that? Would this not have happened to me had I not drowned them, had I not shown such cruelty by twirling them on their tails and squeezing them hard as I threw them into the water?

And then I remembered the big fish I'd caught by throwing myself down on it—how it thrashed about on the pebbles when I threw it there, and how it gasped for water by opening and closing its mouth with the big fat lips and its gills, and how desperately it struggled, trying to free itself as I was holding it down while hitting it with the stone.... I'd been a monster then and no wonder I was finding myself in this situation. I was being punished for having been one!

*You realized?*

But then I realized how silly it was to think such thoughts. Nobody watches secretly over what you're doing, and there's no one like that to punish or reward you for your deeds. The same thing would have happened to me had I thrown the fish back into the water or let the kittens live. I was finding myself in that situation because I'd missed the train, and I was on the train because there was a war, and I'd missed it because I was a dreamer and there was no one to watch over me, and there was no one to watch over me because my mother had died and my father went away to fight the Russians.

*No difference?*

But whether or not I was being punished made no difference. It was the situation I was facing that mattered. What I had to deal with was the present, and not the past.

*You thought?*

What would happen to me? I thought. I was finding myself in the middle of nowhere in a foreign country, among people whose language I didn't speak and who'd generally been hostile to us. I remembered hearing stories how Hungarians soldiers had treated Ukrainian peasants—*badiky*—during the preceding war—how they'd festooned roads with hanging them on the trees growing along their sides. I couldn't expect kind treatment from them. Would they send me back home? It was probably under the Russians now, and if not now, then very soon, so they couldn't do it. Would they put me into an orphanage, for me to become a Hungarian? Would I become a servant-slave on some Hungarian farm? None of the possibilities were any good.

*Hungarian woman?*

The image of the Hungarian woman who'd smiled at me in the market hall then popped up in my mind. Should I try finding her? To become her lover? —It was ridiculous. I was still a child, and even if I were an adult—my father—it wasn't certain we would become lovers. Women like to flirt around, but for many of them a secure marriage, even if not to exactly the right man, is more important than a handsome lover. It was silly to think of the woman as someone who could help me.

*Like dying?*

It is said that when you die, the whole life flashes in an instant before your eyes. There are other times like that too—it took no more than a few seconds for me to think all I've enumerated above.

*Blood thumping?*

My eyes were still on the train, and I could see it getting smaller and smaller, determined at all cost to reach that vanishing point on the horizon it craved so much to be, and thought I could hear the sound its wheels were making on the rails, although it was probably blood thumping in my ears.

*Your hair stood on end?*

It was then that I understood that my situation was desperate and that I didn't know what to do.

Yuriy Tarnawsky

For an instant I thought though I was wrong. There was one thing I'd forgotten about—I could scream! I dismissed the thought immediately however. That wouldn't change anything. It was no better than doing nothing.

And, turning cold once again, I felt the hair on my head stand on end.

# Variation

_____

*Sleep, baby, sleep!*
*Your daddy is a creep.*
*Your mommy is a wicked witch.*
*She makes you sleep in a roadside ditch.*
*Sleep, baby, sleep!*

# A checklist of JEF titles

JEF
Journal of
Experimental
Fiction

www.ingramcontent.com/pod-product-compliance
Lightning Source LLC
Chambersburg PA
CBHW020759250626
47155CB00003B/1142